UNDERCOVER LOVE

UNDERCOVER LOVE

•

Mary Sydney Burk

AVALON BOOKS
NEW YORK

Published by Thomas Bouregy & Co., Inc.
160 Madison Avenue, New York, NY 10016

Library of Congress Cataloging-in-Publication Data

Burk, Mary Sydney.
    Undercover love / Mary Sydney Burk.
        p. cm.
    ISBN 978-0-8034-7763-6 (acid-free paper)   1. Drug
enforcement agents—Fiction.   2. Undercover
operations—Fiction.   3. Farm life—Fiction.   I. Title.
    PS3602.U7535U53 2010
    813'.6—dc22
                                                    2009054250

PRINTED IN THE UNITED STATES OF AMERICA
ON ACID-FREE PAPER
BY HADDON CRAFTSMEN, BLOOMSBURG, PENNSYLVANIA

Chapter One

Lydia slowly flipped through the pages of the cookbook she had pulled from the shelf in her friend Sophie's bookstore, mildly interested in the one hundred and one ways to prepare chicken. Not that she cooked very often. She smiled as she thought about it. Her survival depended more on fast food and take-out than on her culinary skills. Having Erin at the farm for the summer meant they would all eat well, even though it was sometimes pretty exotic. Erin, at fourteen, was aspiring to be a chef and someday own her own restaurant, and her aunt and her twin brother were her designated guinea pigs for the summer.

When Lydia heard the click of the lock and realized the lights were out, she turned and watched Sophie walk toward her. Sophie was grinning and pointing at the book Lydia was holding. "No way! You're not going to take up cooking, are you?"

"Absolutely not." Lydia grinned. "Erin and Eric are here for the summer. Erin's doing the cooking."

"That's good to know," Sophie said, smiling. "So, what are you doing in town at this time of day? It can't be to see my charming self, can it?"

Lydia laughed, pushing the book back onto the shelf among the hundred or so other cookbooks that Sophie stocked. "How can the world be so concerned with cooking? Look at all these books! All on the same subject!"

Sophie rolled her eyes. "Just because you're a lousy cook and totally disinterested, doesn't mean everybody else is. You're the one who grows some of the food these people like to cook. How's the garlic crop, anyway?" she asked, sitting down in one of the comfortable armchairs that she had scattered throughout the store.

"It looks good. We cut all the scapes off weeks ago and the leaves are browning off. It'll be ready to pull by the middle of the month. I'll bring some when it's ready," Lydia replied as she flopped into another chair, lifting one foot to lay her ankle on her other knee. She started to scrape a patch of mud off her calf with her thumbnail, not paying attention to the dried dirt that landed on the tiled floor.

Sophie leaned back, watching. The air conditioner compressor kicked on, increasing the background noise. The day had been hot and Sophie admitted that she was glad she had spent the money to upgrade the cooling system. Customers who were comfortable tended to browse more, and in the end, bought more books. It didn't take a business genius to figure the benefits, she thought.

Lydia looked up, grinning. "I'll clean up the mess, Sophie. I probably tracked some mud in on my sneakers too. Sometimes I forget where my feet have been before I come into town."

"Don't worry," Sophie said, waving one hand negligently. "The cleaning crew will get it when they come in." She looked at the faint scratches on Lydia's forearms. "Is the hay all in, so your arms can heal up?" she asked, pointing at the red marks on her friend's arms.

Lydia looked at the web of scratches and puncture marks and laughed, gently scratching the tiny scabs. "I know I should wear long sleeves when we're unloading hay, but it's always too hot. I'd rather get poked by the cut edges of the hay then be any hotter than I usually am. Anyway," she continued, "we're almost done. I baled up the last of it this afternoon, before I came into town, and the kids will help unload it tomorrow morning, when it's cooler. I'll be glad when it's done. This hay season has stretched out too long because of all the rain we had in June. At least none of the machinery has broken down while Dad's away. That's a relief, anyway." She sighed.

"So what's really on your mind, Lyddy?"

"You're in town all the time," Lydia said. "Is there much drug activity going on?"

Sophie blinked. "Trust you to spring that kind of a question out of nowhere." She watched Lydia flip some more mud off her leg and said, "There is some that I know of. I've seen some deals here in town. You know, a hand reaching out a car window to the car pulled up next to it, money changing hands, a little package in exchange. And the kids who come in here talk. They know what's going on. They don't say anything to me directly, but I hear things, you know?"

"You're saying it's more than a little marijuana?"

"Even a little marijuana is too much, but here, in this area, it's seems to be more underage drinking that goes on in the high school crowd. I don't know what's happening over at the college. I doubt its lily white over there," she said dryly, "but I don't have as much contact with them. They don't spend their money in here." She paused, watching her friend. "Across the river, they seem to have a much bigger problem with hard drugs. The wall in front of the high school is the place to go if you want to buy something illicit. Everybody in the city knows it. The city cops patrol the sidewalk in front of the wall and that doesn't stop it."

Lydia put her foot on the floor and leaned forward, resting her forearms on her thighs. "Erin and Eric told me it's pretty much the same at their school. They know who the kids are that are doing it but nothing much seems to happen to change things. The teachers know, the cops know, but it still happens."

"I doubt it will change until the supply is cut off. And that means making it unprofitable for the farmers to grow it and more profitable to grow something else. How that's going to happen, I don't know," Sophie admitted. "What got you going on this subject, anyway?"

Lydia leaned back in her chair, stretching her legs out in front of her. "Maybe it's nothing, but there's been a seaplane landing at the airport next to the farm." She paused, studying the tips of her sneakers.

"And?" Sophie prompted.

"And it lands every three days, at the same time in the afternoon, and takes off again in fifteen minutes. I noticed it when I got home this spring. The pattern never varies. And, a couple of times, I've seen a black SUV coming out of the old access road next to the runway, early in the morning, and each time, it's been the morning following a visit from the seaplane."

"Maybe the plane is a commuter job, and maybe the SUV is full of hunters sizing up the area for next deer season," Sophie said, raising her eyebrows.

"Maybe. But a seaplane? And what would anybody commute to up here? This isn't exactly corporate nirvana, you know. That little airport isn't very busy, and this seems too much like a pattern to me. Anyway," she added, "it made me suspicious and I wondered if you had noticed anything here in the village." Lydia frowned and reached down to brush more dirt off her legs. "I called my uncle a few days ago. He said he'd pass the information on to the right people at the DEA."

"I forgot your uncle retired from that agency. Is he coming up this summer?"

"Later this month, after Mom and Dad get back from their travels. He likes to get out of Annapolis for a few weeks when it gets really hot down there." She stood up, straightening her T-shirt. "I'd better get home. I left Erin making dinner and Eric shooting baskets in the machinery shed. Thanks for lending an ear, Soph," Lydia said, moving toward the front door.

"Anytime," Sophie said, walking ahead to unlock the door. She stopped suddenly, and Lydia caught her arm to keep from knocking into her. "Who is *that*?" Sophie breathed.

Lydia looked around her, seeing a tall, blond man looking at the displays in the store windows. His khaki pants had a knife-edged crease and the pressed, sapphire blue shirt he wore was the same color as the eyes that were now studying Sophie. He smiled then, the creases at the corners of his eyes deepening, before he winked at her. He turned away from the window and strolled toward the corner.

"My goodness. I think I'm having a hot flash!" Sophie said, waving a hand in front of her face. "He's about the best-looking thing I've ever seen in this town."

"And you've been looking, I guess?" Lydia asked.

"Well, duh, of course." Sophie grinned.

Sophie was patting her chest with one hand and waving the other in front of her face when Lydia stepped in front of her, opened the dead bolt, and let herself out the door. "Down, girl," she called over her shoulder as she pulled the door shut behind her, laughing.

The heat seemed more intense as she walked to the SUV she had driven to town. Lydia turned the air-conditioning on high once she had started the engine. She sat there, letting the heat dissipate, watching the blond in the pressed khakis saunter along the sidewalk. She had never seen him before, which didn't mean a whole lot, she thought. She was away at graduate school for most of the year, so it wouldn't be unusual for her not to know every newcomer in town.

He turned the corner, moving out of sight, and Lydia glanced in the side mirror before she pulled away from the curb. She tooted the horn at Sophie as she passed the bookstore, and turned at the corner. She recognized the blond hair of the driver who pulled out in front of her, and noted the nondescript sedan he was driving.

The village was small and there was very little traffic at this hour, though Lydia had noticed more traffic on the streets, more luxury SUVs than dirty pickups. Even the pickups looked new, which was amazing considering the farm economy. There were new houses popping up all over the county, though, built on land that had recently been farmland, and some of those new trucks sported signs for building contractors, plumbers, electricians, and painters.

Lydia sighed as she passed another farm with a bulldozer and an excavator sitting in a field, the cows gone and the fences falling down. The daughters had sold the farm when Hubey had died two years ago. They didn't want the farm and their own children weren't interested in working seven days a week, outside in any weather, dependent on the vagaries of cattle and milk prices. Now there would be houses and mini-estates dotting the pastures and hayfields, and the new owners would wonder what had happened to all the beautiful open space that had attracted them to the area.

Ten minutes later, Lydia pulled behind the farmhouse and parked in the shade of a sugar maple. She heard the sound of a plane approaching the airport to the east as she walked toward the screened porch. The sound was so very different from the roar of the seaplane that she barely glanced at it. Tomorrow should bring another visit from that plane, if it kept to its pattern. Maybe she would call her uncle again.

Chapter Two

The car turned in at the farm gate and moved slowly along the lane until it reached the shade of some tall locust trees. Dan Madison sat for a minute, watching a young girl pull bales of hay down from the small mountain at the back of the wagon and toss each one toward a woman, standing on the forward drop gate, who threw bale after bale into the interior of the barn.

The little cloud of dust that had followed his car down the lane caught up and rolled gently over the vehicle, leaving another layer of dirt coating the dull brown paint and drifting in through the open window. Although he was accustomed to the lack of amenities in his vehicle, it didn't stop him from wishing for air-conditioning.

A black-and-white dog, lying in the shade under

the wagon, raised her head from her paws and watched him get out of the car. She didn't bark or move toward him, just continued to pant gently in the early morning heat.

Lydia's eyes were stinging and she wiped her forehead with her bare arm. She was sweating heavily, rivulets running down her back and fat droplets dripping off her nose. That was a good thing, she thought, as she sent another bale of hay sailing through the air into the darkness. The heat had moved in like a heavy blanket before they had gotten half the hay unloaded and stacked in the barn. She winged another bale into the darkness of the barn and heard her nephew Eric's grunt as he caught it in midflight. She couldn't be dehydrated yet, she reminded herself. She swung around, reaching for the strings on the bale Erin had rolled toward her from the back of the wagon. The sweat trickling down between her shoulder blades left an itchy trail that begged for relief. Somehow, she thought, it always seemed to be the hottest day of the year when the hay had to be stacked in the barn.

Erin stopped sending bales toward her, and Lydia straightened up before she turned to check on her niece. "You okay?"

"Yeah, but there's a gorgeous guy standing under the trees, watching us." She sighed dramatically. "I wish I was ten years older."

Lydia turned around, again wiping her forehead on

the back of her arm. The dusty car pulled into the shade near the barn wasn't remarkable. The tall man standing next to it surely was. He was dressed in faded jeans and a black T-shirt that stretched across his impressive chest. His dark brown hair was a little long and curled against his neck. Both Erin and Eric stopped working.

Lydia could see her border collie get up from her place in the shade and move out from under the wagon. The dog's eyes were fixed on the man by the car. Lydia knew that Flirt's stare could intimidate most strangers.

After looking around, the man started toward them, continuing to scan the area as he walked. The dog followed him with her eyes but didn't move. He didn't look like a lamb buyer, but you never knew, Lydia thought.

Lydia could hear Erin sigh and mumble "Mm-hmm" as she watched him approach. One corner of his mouth quirked upward as he looked at Lydia. She straightened and smiled in welcome. "How can I help you? We don't have any lambs for sale at the moment, if that's what you're looking for."

His dark brown eyes stared up at her for a minute before his smile widened. "This is Glennmont Farm, isn't it?"

"Yup," Lydia drawled, even as she wondered why she sounded like Billy Denzel, the hired man up at Irv's farm. "I'm Lydia Glenn," she added.

He stepped closer. "My name is Dan Madison. My folks live near your uncle Mark in Annapolis and mentioned that you might have a cottage to rent. I'm going to be in the area for a month or so and need a place to stay." His smile widened, projecting sincerity, and Lydia wondered why she thought he was overdoing it.

She sat down on a bale of hay as she contemplated the man standing just below her. She could see that his eyes were brown—deep chocolate brown—and there were fine lines next to them. He was probably in his early thirties. There was a faint dimple in his left cheek that made him look almost boyish.

Erin was nudging her and murmuring, "Say yes." Eric looked over at her and nodded. "The tenant cottage is empty, Lydia."

Lydia turned to look at them, her eyebrows raised. They were both grinning at her and she knew they had been listening to her own mother. Her mother would be happy to see her attached to some "nice young man" before she got too much older. Hey, she wasn't even thirty yet, she had thought when she overheard the conversation. She rolled her eyes and turned to look at the man standing patiently a few feet away.

"Well, you guys, let's take a break and get something to drink," she said, and promptly swung herself down off the wagon, landing with a little puff of dust as her sneakers hit the dry ground. "You go on up to the house. Mr. Madison and I will be there in a minute."

She turned toward the man standing in front of her and gestured with her head toward an overturned water tank in the shade. She strode toward it and he followed, thinking that jeans and T-shirts must have been designed with her in mind. She certainly filled them well, Dan thought. She was slender and four or five inches shorter than his own six feet and moved with confidence. He could see the dark perspiration stain reaching down the back of her T-shirt to where it was tucked into the waistband of her jeans. Her sneakers were old and ratty looking and she had no socks on. Her light brown hair was streaked with gold and pulled back in a ponytail, showing her slender neck.

Lydia lowered herself onto the edge of the water tank and leaned back on her hands, blowing her breath upward.

Dan had the urge to brush the hair back from her face and he stuffed his fists in his jeans pockets to stop himself. She looked hot and tired, and he wanted to do something to make her work easier. As if he knew anything about farming, he thought, shaking his head slightly. He sat on the other end of the water tank, realizing that the dog had taken up a position in the shade, watching him with an unblinking stare.

Lydia looked at him for a few seconds, her gaze steady, obviously appraising him. "So you know Uncle Mark and Aunt Daisy."

He stared at her for a second, getting the feeling that she was testing him. "I know Mark, but not your aunt. Is her name really Daisy?"

"No, it's not."

"So, you were testing me. I wonder why." Dan smiled at her, but he didn't coax a smile in return. He wondered when he'd lost his touch. Maybe during months of undercover work. Maybe this woman just had better instincts than most.

He had done a background check on her and knew she was in graduate school and had two brothers in the U.S. Navy. Her uncle had retired from the Drug Enforcement Administration three years ago and he knew Mark would verify his story if she checked with him. He didn't want word to get around a small community like this that his visit here was related to anything other than a need for quiet while he finished writing a book.

"So, what's your reason for needing a place for the next month?" Lydia asked. "This is not exactly a vacation mecca."

"I'm looking for a place with no distractions so I can finish a book. I'm up against a deadline," he confided, giving her a smile.

He realized that she didn't look convinced and watched as she turned her head to examine his car. She looked back at him and smiled. Her smile looked just a little incredulous.

"You know, that car you're driving looks an awful lot like the ones that my uncle used to drive. You know: nondescript, unobtrusive, invisible."

Dan thought she was too observant and probably too smart to fool for long. He gave it his best shot though.

"Struggling writer, you know," shrugging his shoulders.

Lydia raised her eyebrows but didn't say anything right away. She turned to look behind her toward a cottage sitting on a slight rise about one hundred yards away. "Okay, you can have it for the month. It will cost you a thousand dollars. There are some furnishings, enough to get by with, and I can loan you sheets and towels, if you need them."

Dan already knew that it contained one bedroom with a queen-size bed, a living room, and a kitchen outfitted with a few pots and pans. He had decided that the cottage on this farm was as perfect as he could hope for. It faced east, overlooking the small airport that was his real interest. The New York office of the DEA had received several reports of suspect activity related to that little airport and his boss thought it was worth investigating. A request from the county Sheriff's Department had further convinced him. He didn't intend to share this piece of information with the woman sitting next to him, but he did intend to pump her and those two teenagers for whatever information they could give him about the activity around the airport.

Dan admired the light brown hair streaked gold by the sun and realized that her gray-blue eyes were studying him. He smiled at her, hoping it would relieve any suspicions she might have, but she just raised her eyebrows again. Oh, well, he thought, since his innocent look wasn't working, he'd have to try something else.

Lydia walked up the hill toward the house, her mind turning over possibilities. She thought he could be telling the truth, or maybe a version of the truth, about his reason for staying in the area. She was conscious of his lean body as he strode easily beside her up the hill. He moved like a runner or maybe just somebody who exercised a lot.

"That's a nice house," he said as they approached the back of a two-story white house with a big screened porch on the side. "A couple of hundred years old, I'd guess."

"Yeah, you're right. The newest part dates from 1831. Come on inside," she added. "The twins will have something ready by now."

Dan followed her up the steps to a back porch and then through a screen door into a slate-floored room, screened all around and furnished with white wicker chairs and a round glass-topped table. The boy and girl he had seen earlier were sprawled in chairs cushioned with thick pillows covered in some kind of floral fabric. It looked comfortable and homey.

"This is my niece, Erin, and nephew, Eric," Lydia said, introducing him. "Mr. Madison is working on a book, right?" she said, looking at him quizzically. Dan thought the girl looked enough like her aunt to be her daughter, except that her hair was black. Her eyes were the same gray-blue color and looked at him with open interest. Her brother, six inches taller and sandy-haired, standing next to her, shook Dan's hand and mumbled a greeting. "They are my brother Rob's kids and are here to help me this summer. My brother is career Navy and deployed for six months and their mother is visiting her grandmother in Ireland."

"I'm Dan Madison," he said, shaking first Erin's hand and then Eric's.

"Help yourself to iced tea or a bottle of water and some of Erin's chocolate chip cookies, if you like," Lydia invited.

"Iced tea is fine for me, thanks," he said, smiling at her. He waited until she sat down and put her feet up on a low table before he took the glass of tea and settled onto a large ottoman. He stared at her bare feet, propped up on the table, and smiled as she wiggled her toes.

It was quiet on the porch and Dan could hear the intermittent sounds of cicadas. The day was hot and he could see that Erin and Eric were slouched in their chairs, looking drowsy.

Erin opened her eyes. "What kind of stuff do you write, Mr. Madison?"

"Actually, I write Westerns."

"You mean like Zane Gray?"

"Yeah, kind of," he admitted.

Erin grinned at him. "Eric reads them all the time. I think he wants to be a cowboy when he grows up."

"Do not," Eric retorted, pushing himself up in his chair and then yawning widely.

Lydia was drinking deeply from a water bottle, her head resting back against the cushions of her chair. She drank until the bottle was empty and then heaved a sigh. "Boy, I needed that," she said. "When you two have had enough to drink," she continued, "go find a set of queen bedsheets and a couple of towels and take them up to the cottage. Make up the bed for Mr. Madison while you're there, okay? I'll meet you at the barn."

"I wish you would all call me Dan. And there's no need to make up the bed. I can do that." He smiled at Erin and Eric and then glanced at Lydia.

Eric stood and yanked up his jeans, saying, "We'll take care of it for you. No problem." He went inside the house, coming back a minute later with a bundle of sheets under his arm. Erin stood up with a groan. "See ya," she said, turning her head to grin at Lydia. She let the screen door bang behind her before she trotted down the steps to catch up with her brother.

"They really are twins, huh?"

Lydia raised her eyebrows. "Sure. Erin gets her black hair from her mother but her eyes are pure Glenn. That color, neither blue nor gray, is dominant in this family and Eric is the spitting image of my brother." She jumped to her feet and said, "Let me take you up to the cottage. There's room to park your car up there and you can unload your stuff when you like. Eric can help you as soon as we get this hay unloaded."

"All right, but I won't need any help unloading. I just have a couple of duffels and my laptop," he said.

Lydia nodded. "Good enough. By the way, the cottage is connected to cable so you have Internet and TV and the phone up there is already connected. Just use a phone card for long distance, if you would."

"Okay," he agreed.

Lydia grabbed a key off a hook by the kitchen door and handed it to her new tenant. "Nobody locks their door around here but here's the key. I have to get back to the barn to help the kids get the hay unloaded, so I'll let you settle in on your own. Call the house if you need anything. The number is next to the phone."

She left him at his car, walking out of the shade into the sunlight as she moved toward the hay wagon. The sun caught the blond streaks in her hair before she pulled a hat out of her back pocket and jammed it on her head. Dan watched until she reached the wagon and grabbed the metal rack to pull herself up.

The hay wagon was almost empty when Lydia hopped up on to the drop gate. Erin was perched up on the stack and Eric was pitching bales at her as quickly as he could grab them up. It was obvious he was trying to knock her down and she was shrieking in protest. "Stop that, you jerk! You're going to wreck this stack!"

Lydia jumped from the wagon up onto the stack, and quickly jammed bales in place. "You hit me with one of those, bozo, and you're dead meat." Lydia laughed, quickly setting bales in place, using her knee to force them tight. "As soon as we get done here, you guys go out and check the sheep," she continued. "Don't forget to take the .22 with you. I'm determined to nail that killer coyote. You both know the rules about shooting so your trajectory is downward."

"Sure, Lyddy, no problem." Eric grinned. He threw the last bale toward Lydia, grinning when she caught it in midair. "Come on, Rin. Let's get this wagon pushed out and hooked up to the quad. We can drop it off in the orchard. Then we can go do some coyote hunting."

"Try not to shoot a sheep, will you?" Lydia warned.

"No problem. We do know that those big white fluffy things are not coyotes. Don't worry," he added. "Those instructors at the safety course we took were crazed about identifying your target."

Erin jogged toward the machinery shed while her brother and Lydia maneuvered the wagon into position. The roar of the quad's engine disturbed some pigeons nesting in the rafters and they soared out of the building in formation, flying in a wide arc above the roof.

Erin backed the quad up to the tongue of the wagon and Eric moved into position and dropped a draw pin in place, securing the wagon to the quad. With Eric on the back, cradling the rifle in his arms, Erin revved up her machine and pulled away slowly. Lydia watched them until they safely made the turn behind the machinery shed and then started to walk back to the house.

She was thinking about grilled cheese sandwiches

for lunch when it occurred to her that her new tenant probably didn't have any food with him to stock the cottage. It wouldn't hurt to invite him for lunch, she thought. It might also give her an opportunity to figure out why he was really here. Maybe she'd call her uncle Mark. She hadn't talked to him or her aunt Susan in a week and maybe she'd just check the guy's reference while she was at it.

She thought about his eyes, comparing their color to the dark chocolate made by a small candy company in the next village. She loved that chocolate. Even though his eyes reflected a cynical view of the world, she thought his default expression was a smile. For someone who looked to be in his early thirties, she suspected he had seen more of the world and its ways than she wanted to know about.

Dan had his few belongings stowed away in the dresser drawers within a few minutes of carrying his duffel bags inside the cottage. He had learned to pack fairly lightly in the years he had spent traveling, living for short periods in various spots around the country. He and his father had fixed up the third floor of his parents' house in Annapolis and he lived in that little apartment when he returned to the East Coast. He sorely missed the Chesapeake Bay waters where he had sailed his first Sunfish.

The phone rang just as he snapped his leather duffel closed. Eric's voice issued an invitation to have lunch with them at the house. "Lydia wondered if there was anything you needed from town. We're making a grocery run this afternoon."

"Thanks for the lunch invite. I'll walk up there in a few minutes, if that's OK. I'm just putting my gear away," he told Eric.

He sat his laptop on the desk in the corner of the living room, next to the phone, and thought that he had better pick up an adapter while he was in town so he could leave the phone and computer plugged in at the same time. He checked to make sure he hadn't left anything in plain sight that he didn't want seen and walked back into the bedroom and retrieved his handgun, placing the Glock in a drawer under a pile of T-shirts. Satisfied, he stepped out the screen door. His eyes did an automatic survey around him before he trotted down the stairs and headed toward the farmhouse.

Eric waved him onto the screened porch as he approached and invited him to sit at the table. "Lydia said to tell you to go ahead and fix yourself something to drink. There's water and iced tea and soda."

The smell of toasted cheese preceded Lydia as she stepped out onto the porch carrying a platter stacked with sandwiches. "This is my specialty—my only specialty," she said as she placed the platter in the center of the table. "I only cook survival and comfort food. It's a good thing Erin likes to cook. None of us like to do dishes, therefore the paper plates and cups."

Dan smiled at her as she sat down across from him.

"I can't cook at all so anything anybody cooks and gives me is welcome."

Lydia raised an eyebrow. "You can't cook at all?"

"I can heat a microwave dinner. Does that count?" he asked.

"I don't think so." She laughed. "Maybe you better plan on eating with us. Erin always makes lots of extras, so you're welcome anytime." She tilted her head at him, saying, "Did I mention that I talked to my uncle Mark today?"

"That was very wise of you to check my references," he said with a trace of a smile tilting the corners of his lips.

"Yeah. He did admit to knowing you and your parents. He spent thirty-five years with the DEA, and he can still do his sphinx act when he wants to. I had the feeling that he was doing that today. I wonder why?" she asked, raising her eyebrows at him.

"I don't know," he said, smiling blandly before he reached for a sandwich.

Chapter Three

Except for the newer houses on the outskirts, every house looked like it dated from the 1829 founding of the village. Small and large, the houses sported metal roofs and wide porches. Flowers filled window boxes, tubs, and hanging baskets that were suspended from porch railings. Huge shade trees towered over the homes lining the village street. The business district extended in four directions from the traffic light in the center of town, with small shops occupying the ground floor of the buildings.

"Lydia, can we stop at the bookstore before we get groceries?" Eric asked from the backseat. "I want to look for a copy of Dan's book."

"Sure," Lydia said, signaling and pulling into a parking place along the main street.

"There's a hardware store right across the street, Dan. Didn't you say you needed to go there?" she asked, turning her head to look at him in the passenger seat next to her.

"Yeah, I did," he replied.

Erin and Eric were scrambling out of the backseat before Lydia turned off the engine. She came around the front of the SUV while Dan climbed out and stood on the sidewalk. He looked across the street and spotted his partner standing in front of the display window of a store with a collection of lawn mowers lined up in front. The crisp white shirt and pressed khakis made him look like a city executive on dress-down Friday.

Lydia pointed down the sidewalk. "The book store is called The Bookworm, down there on the right. Don't hurry. We'll be there awhile. Books are my one extravagance." She smiled as she turned away and started walking. She had changed from jeans to shorts and Dan watched her lean, lightly tanned legs, admiring the smooth flex of muscle as she moved away.

He dragged his attention back to the hardware store and shook his head slightly as he acknowledged that his partner would never dream of compromising his yacht club persona by dressing like a local. Kevin played the role of dilettante very well.

Dan crossed the street and entered the store. A quick glance showed him a counter with a register manned by two teenagers who were laughing and poking each other in the ribs. Nobody else was in sight.

Moving down the center aisle, he quickly located what he was looking for among the telephone accessories. He paid for it and stepped out of the store, nodding slightly to his partner who was climbing into his car parked on the other side of the street, his blond hair shining in the brilliant sun light.

Dan walked in the other direction until he was opposite the bookstore, then crossed the street in front of a pickup truck that had stopped and whose driver waved him across.

A bell jangled as he opened the door, but otherwise it was quiet inside. He wandered through the rows of paperbacks toward the rear of the store and found Lydia sitting in a comfortable armchair, reading. She looked up when he pulled a chair out from the table in the middle of the floor and moved it toward her.

"You're really lucky to have a bookstore in such a small town, aren't you?" he asked as he sat down.

"Yes, very," she agreed. "There's a big chain store about twenty-five miles away and I admit to buying a lot of books over the Internet, but I personally love a bookstore and the feel and smell of the books. My high school aptitude tests indicated I was suited to be a librarian, but I think that was because I loved to read." She frowned. "I also think those tests were gender biased."

Smiling, Dan admitted, "I can't see you as a librarian. You look more like the outdoor type."

"Well, I am. Lab work bores me, which is why my

thesis is based on something that takes me outside a laboratory," she agreed.

"What do you read when you're not being academic?" he asked.

She grinned. "Sorry, it's not Westerns! Mostly I read mysteries. Not too violent, though. Those give me nightmares, so I stick with cozies and the lighter ones."

"Truthfully, I don't read a lot of fiction myself. Most of the stuff I read is background material for a book. You know, history, the geography of an area, social treatises about an era I'm interested in." He shrugged. "I don't have too much time for anything else."

"Is that because your regular job keeps you busy?"

When he looked startled, she added, "Remember, I talked to my uncle this morning. And I should tell you that I talked to my uncle about the activity at the airport weeks ago."

"O-kaaay. I guess my cover is blown," he said, smiling. "I thought you didn't exactly believe my story."

She shook her head. "No. Your cover isn't blown. Nobody knows anything, really. I just happened to remark to my uncle about the unusual activity in and out of the airport and, the next thing I know, you show up with a pretty thin story." She looked at him and saw him frowning and added, "The kids don't think anything of it. By the way, Eric found your book and is already reading it over there by the coffee machine," indicating another armchair at the other side of the room in which Eric was sprawled.

He continued to frown at her. "I don't want you to know anything about this or be involved in any way, understand?"

"Yes, sir. Whatever you say, sir." She nodded, allowing a smile to spread across her face. "Let's get this show on the road. I mean the grocery shopping, of course," she said as she stood up, giving him an innocent look.

"Of course," he repeated, placing a hand on her arm. "Just don't forget what I said."

She didn't answer as she walked over to Eric. "Hey, we've got to get moving," she said. "Find Erin. I think she's in the cookbook section. Tell her I'm ready to go as soon as I pay for whatever books you want."

Their foray in the grocery store produced twelve bags to be loaded into the back of the SUV.

"I try to come into town only once a week," Lydia remarked as she lowered the back gate of the vehicle, having noted the surprised look on Dan's face at the quantity of food they had bought. "There's enough here for you, so consider yourself invited for dinner every day."

She looked over at him as she slid into the driver's seat. "The cornflakes, milk, and frozen dinners you bought wouldn't sustain me for very long."

Erin leaned forward from the backseat. "Please come. I can try out some new recipes on you. Lydia isn't very adventurous when it comes to food."

Dan looked over his shoulder at her. "Sorry, neither am I. I pretty much stick with steak and potatoes, if I have a choice." He smiled at her look of disappointment. "Don't worry. I'll eat anything you offer rather than cook for myself."

"You must know how to cook something," Lydia said.

"Well, yeah," he admitted. "I can grill a steak and bake a potato in the microwave."

"That's not much of a repertoire," Lydia teased.

"Wait a minute." He laughed. "The way I hear it, you don't do much better."

"Not so," she answered. "I can cook spaghetti, pot roast, and tuna-noodle casserole."

There was a groan from the backseat. "Run for cover if that tuna-noodle thing shows up on the dinner table," Eric said. "That's pretty much all we ate until Erin took over the cooking."

"No way," Lydia protested with a laugh. "You're maligning me here, Eric. I'm sure I cooked something else!"

"Not so," Erin chimed in, siding with her brother. "You have to admit I'm a better cook than you are."

"No contest." She grinned. "My theory is that if someone else is willing to do it, go for it. Besides," she added, "I've been busy doing other stuff."

Dan grinned, enjoying their banter. "So I take it Lydia and I are excused from kitchen duty."

"Only from the cooking," Lydia stated firmly.

"However, the downside is that we get to clean up the mess that Erin makes."

"Hey, I'm a creative genius," Erin explained. "I can't be bothered with the more mundane things of life." She giggled.

"Wait a minute here," Dan said, turning around to look at Eric. "I haven't heard your name in this roster of duties." He raised his eyebrows in question.

"Don't worry," Lydia answered him. "I assigned him laundry duty!"

Eric just shrugged. "You do what you gotta do to keep peace. I'm outnumbered, anyway."

They were slowing down to turn into the farm driveway and Lydia glanced at Dan, saying, "I'll drop you off at the cottage. Dinner's around seven, as soon as we get the evening chores done. Come to the house whenever."

"Thanks. I'll be there," he replied, climbing out and retrieving his bag of groceries from the back. He lifted a hand toward the car as Lydia put it in gear and drove away.

Chapter Four

Three days of watching for a pattern in the take-off and landings at the small airport east of the farm had yielded practically nothing helpful. There weren't more than a dozen landings on any one day. They were all small craft and only one had taken off again within fifteen minutes of landing. That one had been a sea-plane, easily distinguished from all the others by the distinct sound of its engines and lumbering take-off. He had seen and heard it only once, on the day he had arrived. It had taken off again within minutes. Unfortunately, he hadn't seen or heard it again.

Knowing that this was mainly an information-gathering assignment didn't make the inactivity any easier to bear. He had used the time to work on the final rewrite of his latest book and that, at least, showed some progress.

He had been walking the lanes around the farm, getting a feel for the way it was laid out, but had resisted the urge to do more than that. He was still establishing his persona as an author on a break from serious writing, on the off chance that anybody was watching him because he was a stranger.

He hoped that the frequent meals he took up at the farmhouse and the easy way Erin and Eric treated him, and his casual pose around the farm would provide enough evidence to anyone watching that he was legitimately vacationing from work and had no other agenda.

He was sure that Lydia knew what he was doing, but she hadn't said anything further. He was glad of that. He didn't want the twins alerted and have them start poking around. They knew this farm very well and he saw them riding around the fields on quads. The cows were pastured on the east side of the farm and the sheep flock appeared to be moved to a new area every day or so. He had walked that way one morning and met Eric as he was maneuvering the sheep through a pulled-back area of the fence. Eric had explained about rotational grazing, which required moving the animals onto a fresh area of pasture every two or three days. Portable electric fencing was used and that meant putting up a new line of fencing around the pasture to be grazed and taking down the fence around the area already eaten down.

Dan thought it sounded like a lot of work and Eric explained that the method extended the grazing season, forced the sheep to eat even the stuff that wasn't their favorite, and actually improved the pasture in the long run. His uncle had set up the system a few years before, Eric had said, and he had been able to expand the size of the flock by extending the amount of forage available. Eric had admitted that, when he had first started doing it, the job had taken him twice as long, but now he could usually do the whole thing in a half hour, unless something went wrong.

Eric had laughed when he told Dan about the day he had forgotten to hook up the solar charger to the new section of fence and the sheep had run right through the wire and dragged it and half the posts for a couple of hundred yards before they quit running and started grazing.

"Of course, I didn't think it was funny at the time and I had to go back and get Lydia and Erin to help," he admitted. "But Lydia is really good with the sheep and she brought old Flirt with her in the truck."

"Who's Flirt?" he asked.

"The border collie that hangs around Lydia. She's pretty old and doesn't work much anymore but she is excellent with moving the flock. She's real calm about it and the sheep seem to know she's in charge. It's kind of funny, actually," he added. "They see her coming and start moving back to where they're supposed to be without a hassle. If I tried to move them, they'd scatter in twenty different directions."

Eric had invited him to hop on the back of the quad while he checked the charge on the fence. Dan did so and after checking the fence with a handheld tester, Eric swung his leg over the quad, revved up the engine, and took off at a good clip.

Dan knocked on the screen door at the kitchen and stepped through the doorway when Erin called out.

"Is your aunt around, Erin?" he asked.

"In the office, hunched over the computer, I think," she replied. "Past the dining room on the right," she continued. "She's been working on the numbers for her dissertation."

Dan passed through the dining room and stopped outside the door of a room that was obviously used as an office. Lydia swiveled her chair around to face him when he tapped on the door frame.

"Hi, Dan. Everything okay?" she asked, smiling.

He returned her smile and Lydia was fascinated by the way that lone dimple appeared in his left cheek. She also noted that the lines at the sides of his eyes deepened as he smiled and her toes practically curled. He was a very good-looking man, she thought, moving her eyes away from that dimple when he spoke.

"I wondered if you had a topographical map or an aerial survey of this area."

"Yes, we have both, if I can just lay my hand on it," she said. She got up and moved over to a file cabinet against the wall. "My dad has a unique system for filing stuff, so this may take a minute."

Dan pulled his attention away from her legs and looked at the curve of her neck as she bent her head over the file folder in her hand. Her slender neck and jaw were exposed by the ponytail holding her hair back from her face. It was a pretty face, he thought, as he brought his eyes further up. Not a beautiful face by classic standards, but a face that was easy to look at.

He brought his attention to her hands as she turned toward him, holding out some sheets of paper. He reached for them, telling himself to keep his mind on his business. She was smiling at him, apparently unaware of his scrutiny.

"Those maps include the airport land and part of the Steiner farm to its north. Why don't I give you the nickel tour of the farm after lunch? We can take one of the quads and get through the woods near the airport. You are interested in getting a look over there, aren't you?" she asked, raising her eyebrows at him.

"Well, yes, but I already told you, you are not to be involved."

"Listen, I live here. Nobody would think anything of my riding a quad around. I do it all the time. And," she added, "I do have to check the cow herd and take a salt block out to them." She grinned at him. "Nothing could be more innocent looking, if anybody was out there watching."

"Okay, okay. It would help if you showed me around. But I'm serious about your minding your own business," he said. "These people are not nice and you don't want to get close to them. Take my word for it."

"Believe me, I intend to stick to my research and leave the skullduggery to you. My goal is to stay 'down on the farm' as long as I can."

Dan followed her out of the room. "Don't you intend to stay in an academic setting?" he asked.

"Nope," she replied over her shoulder. "I've finished all the course work I need. I should have enough data after this summer to finish up my dissertation. If the information I gather in the next couple of months confirms my hypothesis, I can complete the Ph.D. and get out of there."

"What exactly are you working on?" Dan asked as they stepped out into the screened porch.

"Hey, Erin," Lydia called back through the doorway. "Are you making sandwiches?"

"Yes. I've made enough for Dan too," she answered.

Lydia looked at Dan. "You'll stay for lunch, won't you?" she asked as she sat down in one of the wicker chairs and put her feet up on the ottoman.

"Yes, sure," he replied. "Thanks. You were going to tell me about your research."

Lydia leaned back in her chair, tilting her head to

stare up at the ceiling. "It started because I like sheep. They're dumb and defenseless and they can drive you crazy, but I've always liked them better than the cows my father raises." She looked over at him where he sat, relaxed and focused on her. She shrugged and continued. "The market for the wool we take off them every year disappeared. That's a result of world conditions as much as it is our inability to provide a clean, uniform crop to the national and international buyers. That, plus the fact that Australia and New Zealand far outproduce us and make it their business to produce fine wool for the textile market, has left the sheep producers in this country without a market for a big by-product of their operations."

Dan interrupted. "What do you mean when you say 'fine' wool? I thought all wool was the same."

"Not at all. Each breed produces its own type of wool. By that, I mean the length of the fiber, the micron diameter of each fiber, its whiteness or its natural color, and several other criteria that a wool buyer considers. It's all wool, with its microscopic structure, but each breed produces wool with unique characteristics. Anyway," she continued after looking at him again to see him still concentrating on her mini-lecture, "the small producers are particularly hard hit. Sale of the wool contributed a significant proportion of the income from raising sheep."

Dan nodded and she grinned at him. "I expected you to be asleep by now or at least looking stunned."

"Hey, no. It's obvious that the economic aspect of sheep raising is driving whatever it is you're studying. So explain some more," he said as he settled more deeply into his chair and raised his feet to the ottoman, barely touching her foot with his as he did so.

She had closed her eyes again. "Dad developed a line of knitting yarn that we produce from the wool raised here plus some we purchase from local sheep farms. The wool that isn't suitable, like from the belly area, has been used to mulch the vegetable garden. I noticed that we could keep the garden weed-free and reduce the need for watering and weeding as long as we kept a certain density and thickness of wool around the plants. They also seemed to grow better and bigger in the areas where we mulched with wool compared with where we mulched with plastic."

"I think I'm getting the picture. You're working to develop a commercial market for a waste product."

"Exactly," she admitted. "The numbers are looking really good so far. Dad already had most of the equipment and setup to get started and has been making felted mats, which I'm using to mulch part of our garlic planting. A friend on the other side of the village is using it on her commercial lavender crop, and a fruit farm just north of here has been using it on strawberry plantings and new apple tree plantings. They're keeping statistics on growth and production and a bunch of other factors I asked them to monitor."

Both Lydia and Dan looked up as Erin stepped out

onto the porch carrying a platter of hamburgers. "Stop the academics for a while, Lydia. Here's lunch. I've got some more stuff coming, but start on these," she said as she laid the platter on the table.

"I could get used to this kind of living," Dan admitted. "A shady porch to lounge around on, food provided by a chef, and good company."

Lydia looked at him quizzically. "Flattery works very well here. Keep it up."

She pulled her chair up to the table and indicated that he should do the same. "Not flattery, simple truth," he said as he sat down at the table.

Eric came to the table with a big basket lined with paper napkins and overflowing with lightly browned potato slices. "Erin's version of garlic french fries," he said. "She says she bakes them with a little olive oil and sprinkles garlic powder on top and swears they're much healthier than regular French fries. That doesn't matter to me," he added. "I just know they taste really good. One of the best things she cooks," he added, loud enough for Erin to hear him.

"Thanks, brother dear. You get to clean up the kitchen as a reward," Erin responded as she came through the door, carrying a pitcher of iced tea and a pile of paper cups. Eric took them from her before he sat down at the table. "Do you want us to take a salt block out to the cows this afternoon, Aunt Lydia? I noticed that they've licked the last one down to a nub."

"Thanks, Erin, but Dan and I can take it with us on

the quad. I'm giving Dan the farm tour this afternoon." She paused, licking ketchup off her fingers. "This heat is making the cows crave salt, so we keep a block of salt mixed with minerals where they can get to it anytime," she said, glancing at Dan.

He realized that he was staring at her as she licked her fingers, and tried to concentrate on what she said. "I'm getting the idea that farming is not for the faint of heart. Does a farmer ever get any downtime?"

"Sure. We just have to fit it in after everything else gets done. At least Dad doesn't keep milk cows. They're a seven-days-a-week, three-hundred-sixty-five-days-a-year proposition. Not for me," Lydia added, shaking her head. "I like to water ski and swim when the weather's right, and downhill ski in the winter, and be able to disappear for a few days without having to find someone to do the milking twice a day. Nope," she added, "I don't want to live like Irv and Kay, our neighbors up the road. Irv's been milking cows for fifty years. They haven't taken a vacation away from the farm in the past thirty years."

"Didn't you say you wanted to stay down on the farm?" Dan quizzed her, smiling.

"On my terms. I forgot to add that," she said, grinning.

A half hour later Dan swung his leg over the back of the quad and settled himself with his thighs hugging Lydia's hips. She started the machine and took off down the farm lane. The sudden acceleration made Dan grab her around the waist and he heard her laugh. "Sorry. I should have warned you."

"No problem," he yelled over the noise of the engine, taking a tighter hold on her hips. The only problem, from his point of view, was the urge to move closer, he thought. She felt strong and warm under his hands and didn't seem to notice his hold on her. She probably had Erin or Eric on the back of her machine fairly frequently and didn't think he was any different.

Lydia tried not to notice that Dan was practically plastered to her back as she made a sharp turn into a field. As she slowed her speed until they were creeping along, she said over her shoulder, "This is where we grow the garlic. The sheep don't eat it and neither do the deer, so it's been a good crop to grow here. From my perspective, it's good because the production numbers are easy to document. From Dad's viewpoint, it's good because it's not labor intensive until harvest."

She cruised up and down the edges of the field, studying the rows of plants. "This will be ready to harvest in another week. See how the leaves are turning brown? Each leaf represents a bulb cover and we like to have at least four green leaves on the plant when we pull it," she explained. "That leaves enough covering on the bulb so when it's cleaned and loses another one or two covers, there're still enough left to keep the cloves from drying out. This is a hard, or stiff, neck variety and it will keep until around Christmas if it's handled right."

"Your dad's idea to grow garlic?" he asked.

"Yeah. A cash crop. He sells a lot of it at one of the local farmers' markets." She laughed. "When the weather's bad, we have something to do indoors— clean garlic!"

"No idle hands around here, I take it," he commented.

"Never," she replied. "And it turned out well for me because it gave me a crop to study that was already well-established here and was easy to document." She revved up the engine and he instinctively tightened his hold on her as she turned out of the field and increased their speed. A dust cloud followed them as she headed over a rise in the ground and started down the incline toward a wide, long pasture.

The dust cloud caught up with them when she stopped by a gate. "Hop off and open the gate, will you, Dan?" she asked over her shoulder. "The passenger gets to open and shut the gates." She grinned at him as he swung the gate inward to allow her to drive the quad through. He closed the gate behind her and climbed back into his seat.

"Did you just make up that rule?" he asked, leaning against her back to speak into her ear over the sound of the engine.

"No, honestly." She laughed. "The passenger always gets the gates, whether it's the quad, or a truck, or whatever. So now," she added, "you know why Erin and Eric argue over who's going to drive."

She had turned the machine and was riding alongside a small stream lined with bushes. "The cattle will be down here, resting in the shade at this time of day. We'll leave the salt block and check out the back rubber."

"You're kidding, right?" he asked. "Cows get their backs rubbed?"

"Not exactly," she admitted as they slowed to a stop. "It's a device filled with insecticide to control the flies, especially the ones around their faces. It helps prevent the spread of pink eye, which can be a big problem in fly season."

She slid off the machine after it stopped and walked around to the back. "You can stay there, Dan. I just need to put this out for the cows," she said, releasing a dull red-colored block from the holder behind him. She hoisted it up and swung it into a large plastic contraption set under the trees. There was a cover above it and Dan could see that it pivoted as Lydia lifted the block and set it inside the receptacle, built so the salt block was protected from the weather but accessible to the cows.

Lydia moved over to a fringed tube suspended between two trees and, after tilting it, unscrewed a cap from one end. After a quick look inside the tube, she recapped it, gave it a good shake and turned toward him. "That's everything here. You ready?" she inquired as she lifted her leg across the seat and mounted the quad.

"Ready for anything," he answered, and grabbed hold of her hips as she sent the quad racing across the field toward another group of trees. She slowed as she approached and turned to run parallel with the trees. "See," she pointed. "The cows are in there, away from the heat and the flies. They'll come out later to graze again."

"Straight out of a Zane Gray novel," he said into her ear. He could see the corner of her mouth turn up but she didn't say anything. She was concentrating on navigating a steep-sided ditch with water running along its bottom. "Hold on," she called as she gunned the quad up the far side.

Lydia was leaning forward, gripping the handlebars as she wrestled the quad up the steep slope. Dan plastered himself to her back to keep from tumbling off the back end as the machine lurched and rocked. He had his arms wrapped around her waist and her hair was tickling his face as they reached the top of the embankment.

"Sorry about that," she said over her shoulder as she brought the machine to a standstill. "This is the quickest way to the sheep pasture."

"Don't mind me," Dan said into her ear. "I enjoyed it."

Lydia flashed a frown at him. "I think it's safe for you to loosen your grip on me now," she said. She didn't wait for any reply, just gunned the engine and started across the field. She felt him slip his hands to her hips, lightly holding on. At least he wasn't pressing up against her like he had been, she thought. Somehow it had seemed kind of intimate, even though she knew it was his response to the rough ride up the bank of the stream.

He hopped off to open the gate onto the lane and waited until she had moved through. He was checking to make sure the latch was secure when he heard the seaplane overhead. The very distinctive roar of its engine told him it was in its landing pattern for the airport. As he climbed back on behind Lydia, he asked, "Can we take a look over on the eastern side of the farm?"

"Sure," she replied, revving the engine. "We just follow this lane."

Three minutes later, she stopped the quad at the edge of a large unfenced field. "The boundary line is about a hundred yards into these trees," she said, pointing toward the east. "Then there's a narrow field that belongs to Irv's farm, before you reach the edge of the airport property. Come on, I'll show you," she said, sliding off the seat and starting into the woods.

Dan realized she was following a faint trail that was weaving through the trees, and a few minutes later they emerged at the edge of a narrow strip of open land. At the far side, a track was visible and when he asked, Lydia replied that it led north until it came out onto the highway. She thought it had been used when this part of Irv's farm was logged twenty years before.

They crossed the open area and Dan noted that there were some fairly fresh tire tracks in the ruts of the old path. The path would certainly make an inconspicuous way in and out of the airport.

Lydia angled off to the south. "I want to show you something," she said. "There's an old hunting cabin not far from here. I think the roof has pretty much collapsed but it might be worth checking out."

"Wait a minute, Lydia. Tell me how to get to it. I told you not to get involved in this."

"Come on, Dan. Just a quick peek so you know the lay of the land."

She was already striding away from him and plunging into some dense brush, forcing him to slow down for a second while he figured out how she had managed to disappear from sight so quickly.

When he caught up with her, she just pointed toward a wooden structure squatting in the woods. It was obvious that the roof had been repaired recently. It was quiet around them when Dan suddenly grabbed her and pulled her against his chest. His head came down toward hers and for an instant she thought he was going to kiss her. His breath warmed her lips as he whispered, "Just in case somebody's watching."

Then he did kiss her. She stiffened and then, as she relaxed onto his chest, the kiss grew harder, more urgent, until she felt him sigh and pull away. He blinked and said, "Oh, damn."

Then he smiled at her. "Sorry about that. I'm trying to make this look like we're innocently strolling in the woods and not spying." He pulled her back into his embrace and kissed her lightly again.

"Come on, look casual," he said and slowly turned them around before releasing her, only to put his arm around her waist and start walking back the way they had come. Ten yards later, he stopped and kissed her again and this time, she lifted her arms around his neck and sank against him.

When she pulled back, she smiled at the bemused expression on his face and said, "How am I doing?"

When they reached the quad, she moved in close to his chest. "Tell me what's going on, or else," she said as she smiled at him and slipped her hands up his chest. Then, she had her hands in his hair and was pulling his head down toward her. "Don't panic," she whispered against his mouth. "I'm just making this look good for anybody watching. But, if you don't tell me," she added, "I'll call my uncle and worm the truth out of him."

"No, you won't," he said as his arms went around her, seemingly of their own volition. "You know he would never give out information." His lips touched hers and his heart rate speeded up again and he almost forgot the reason they were doing this. They were pretending, weren't they?

She started to move away at the same time he lowered his arms.

"My, oh my," she breathed.

"Let's get out of here," he said, turning her toward the quad. After she settled in the seat, he threw his leg over and slid on behind her. His thighs hugged her hips and his hands reached around her waist as she started the engine.

Lydia could feel the heat of his hands through the thin cotton of her T-shirt and looked over her shoulder to grin at him before she shifted into gear and sent the quad flying over the ground. When she pulled up at the gate onto the lane, she stopped the engine. Before he could dismount, she twisted in her seat and said, "I'll show you how to drive this thing, if you like. You'll be much more mobile around here if you have wheels."

She slid off the seat and opened the gate. When she came back, he had already started the engine and was moving forward. She stepped to the side as he guided the quad through the opening and she quickly closed the gate behind him. As she stood next to him to describe the various features, she couldn't help but notice the muscles bulging in his forearms as he gripped the handlebars.

He looked like he lifted weights, she thought. God, she didn't know anything about him and she had been kissing him like a long-lost lover. She looked away from his forearms to see him looking at her. His expression was serious but his eyes were bright. "This sure has been a good day for me so far. How about you?" he asked.

She had to smile. "Yeah," she admitted. "For me too."

"Well, come on, then," he said. "I know how to drive one of these things. I've been watching you very closely and you can always tell me if I'm doing something wrong."

"Yeah, I can," Lydia muttered, wondering if he was referring to driving the quad or to something else, or maybe both. She climbed on behind him and wrapped her arms around his waist. "I'm ready. Let's go."

Chapter Five

Dan's car was gone from its place next to the cottage when Lydia and Eric finished the evening chores. "You go on down and check the sheep, Eric. I'm going to check the garlic."

When Eric had roared off on his sheep-checking ride, Lydia walked down to the garlic beds. All the plots looked good this year. The leaves were browning off and another few days would see them to harvest. She pulled a few bulbs from each plot and brushed them free of dirt. The aboveground appearance of the plants didn't interest her as much as the condition of the bulbs underground. One plot was mulched with plastic, one with straw and one with wool. They would harvest each plot separately and hang the plants to dry.

Lydia reflected that garlic had been a fairly easy crop to incorporate in the research for her dissertation. She and her father were experienced in its growing habits and cultivation and the harvest was measurable. The data entering and the actual computations were her least-favorite part of this project. Walking along the gardens at the end of the day, just looking at the plants, admiring their growth and planning the next crop was more satisfying. She would be glad when she was finally finished with this part of the research.

It had been easy to gain the cooperation of several other local growers in using the wool product her family had developed. The addition of several other crops to her database had been necessary to provide convincing evidence for the widespread usefulness of wool as a mulching medium. She had recruited a commercial strawberry operation, an apple farmer, and an organic herb farm to get the necessary data.

Their own vegetable garden had been mulched with wool for years. She had done some early investigations on soil temperature with and without mulch before she ever started this project. If her findings proved the usefulness of a wool-based mulch, every organic gardener in the country would cheer, and every sheep farmer in the nation would benefit.

The use that she was envisioning would bypass the need for uniformity and provide a market for the fleeces from the many breeds of sheep found in the country, not just the fine wool breeds that supplied the commercial buyers' needs for wool suitable for fabric for the fashion industry.

Her stomach gave a loud growl just as Flirt ambled over and nudged her leg. "Okay, time for dinner," she said and started out of the garden with the dog trotting ahead of her. Being late for dinner was not an option in Flirt's life.

She checked the tomato plants as she passed and saw that even the earliest varieties were nowhere near ripening. A fresh garden tomato would have tasted really good with dinner, she thought. The beans needed to be picked again, though. She would come back after dinner and do that, she decided.

They had had so much rain this spring and early summer that it hadn't been necessary to water the vegetable garden so far. Everything looked lush after the two previous years when it had been so dry that the little creeks had dried up by the end of June and the pond had dropped three feet over the summer. It would be interesting to see if there was any measurable effect of natural versus artificial watering on the garlic crop. That could add an interesting little sidebar in her research paper.

She had started back toward the house when she saw Dan's car pull in the driveway. She waved at him and changed direction, walking slowly toward the cottage.

She saw him get out of the car and reach back in and grab a couple of bags off the front seat. He turned toward her, holding up the bags, and smiled. "Dessert," he said. "I told Erin I would stop and get it on the way from town."

"I bet it's soft ice cream," she laughed.

"You're right," he admitted.

"It's her favorite. Did you bring some of their strawberry sauce?" she asked as she reached him.

"Of course. That's a necessity, isn't it?" He grinned.

"Well, to me it is," she said. She turned to walk with him as he moved toward the house. "What were you up to in town?" she asked, looking at him quizzically. "And don't try to tell me that you were just going to the bookstore," she added.

"Naw. I went to the hardware store," he said.

She thought he had that guileless look down pat and told him so. "Were you meeting your contact or something?" she asked.

"Come on, Lydia. You know I'm not going to tell you anything about anything, so quit probing." He grabbed her hand with his free hand and laced his fingers with hers.

She didn't pull her hand loose but gave him a look that warned him that she wasn't going to give up. He knew that she thought she could help him because she knew the area so well, and knew the location of every little deer trail, creek, and swamp. But these people didn't play nice and he didn't want her or Erin or Eric anywhere near them.

Dan left as soon as the dinner dishes were done, claiming that he had to catch up on some work. He had refused Eric's invitation to watch a movie with him, thanked Erin for dinner, and waved a casual hand at Lydia as he started down the lane to the cottage.

Lydia was spraying herself with mosquito repellent before she went to the garden to pick beans, as she thought about it. There had been a little more tension in Dan than usual, all through dinner. She admitted that she was sorry he didn't stay for a while as he had done other nights. She suspected that when he mentioned having work to do, it wasn't writing a novel. She had noticed that the seaplane had roared overhead on its approach to the airport when she had been out with Dan that afternoon. Thinking back, she realized that this was the third day since its last appearance and she was sure that Dan was aware of the pattern of its appearances.

She hadn't seen him leave the cottage, but just as it was becoming too dark to see the beans on the plants, realized he was coming into the garden. He had a small canvas bag slung over one shoulder, and he swung it to the ground as he came through the gate.

As he came up to her, he sniffed and said, "Bug repellent! I knew I was missing something."

Lydia laughed. "After all the rain we've had this season, you should know better than to be out and about at this time of day without major protection. Not that it helps much with the deer flies." She tilted her head and asked, "Did you have much trouble with them where you were? They're especially trouble-some near the east woods." She stepped close and in-spected a couple of large welts on his neck. "Maybe you should put some ice on these," she suggested as she touched first one, then the other.

"It's too dark to be picking beans, Lydia. How can you see the damage those nasty buggers caused?" he asked, rubbing his neck.

Lydia grinned. "Good night vision," she said. "I also know from personal experience how persistent they are and how they hurt when they get you. Did they keep buzzing your head the whole time?"

"Pretty much," Dan admitted. He wasn't surprised that Lydia had figured out where he had been, and was grateful that she hadn't tried to follow along. He had found a set of fresh tire tracks on the old logging road, which didn't mean much, he thought, since every local probably knew about the track, and by the time he had gotten there, everything was quiet. He had met Kevin at the end of the dirt road, close to the highway. Kevin had watched the arrival of the plane and watched it being refueled. After the plane had taxied away and taken off, a man in dirty jeans and a ragged T-shirt had strolled down the edge of the runway and stopped at the fuel pump. He had fumbled with the nozzle of the pump for a minute, and Kevin saw a panel on the side open up. A bag was shoved inside his shirt, the panel closed, and then the guy had strolled back along the edge of the blacktop for one hundred yards before veering off the edge and disappearing in the woods.

The pickup man, they agreed, looked like a local farmhand. It would make sense to use someone familiar to have a legitimate reason for being near the airport. That narrowed it down to the workers on Irv's farm and the dairy farm just to the south of the airport.

Kevin had searched the hunting cabin after the plane's departure and had found nothing unusual. At this point, it looked like the cabin was not the initial hiding place, and the drop-off must be stowed elsewhere temporarily before being moved there for pickup by the buyer.

Lydia bent to pick up the basket at her feet. It was overflowing with string beans. She showed it to Dan, saying, "This will keep me busy for a while. I love growing the stuff and being able to eat it during the winter, but I'm not that thrilled with all the work involved in getting it into the freezer."

She walked through the gate and then turned and waited while Dan retrieved his pack from the ground. When he bent over, she noticed a bulge under the back of his shirt and instantly realized he had a gun stuck in the waistband of his jeans.

When he straightened up and turned back toward her, she said, "Do you want to come back to the house after you get rid of the tools of your trade? You could help us string these beans since you'll probably be eating some of them. We eat a lot of beans when the crop is ready, like it is now. Pretty soon we'll be sick of them and then more of it makes its way to the freezer while we start pigging out on whatever is next in season."

"Sure, I'll do that," he replied

A few minutes later, he dumped his pack on the bed of the cottage and pulled his shirt over his head. He eased the Glock from his waistband and slid it into the dresser drawer, realizing as he pulled some T-shirts over it that Lydia had noticed it. It hadn't seemed to startle or alarm her. Growing up in the country had probably made her familiar with firearms.

He had spent hours on the firing range, keeping up skills that could become rusty from disuse. There were times in his career when he sat around pushing paper and working a computer and it was too easy to lose the edge necessary for survival out in the field. He considered himself fortunate that he seldom was called on to actually take down a suspect with anything other than brute force or stealth, but the knowledge that he was well-trained and very skilled with his weapon was reassuring.

After he changed his jeans for a pair of khaki slacks and pulled a clean shirt over his head, he glanced around to make sure his equipment was put away. Kevin was settled in to watch the hunting shack and Dan would relieve him at two in the morning. He could spend some time with Lydia and the twins, then get a couple hours' sleep before he had to take over the watch. This time, he assured himself, he would be well protected against those crazy insects that seemed to think they owned the woods!

Lydia was sitting on the wicker settee in the darkened porch when Dan approached the house. She was snapping the ends off the beans, filling the basket in her lap, and letting the finished ones drop into a big metal pot resting next to her on the cushions.

Erin stuck her head out the kitchen door as he stepped onto the slate floor and smiled at him in greeting. "You almost done there, Lydia? The water's boiling in the steamer."

"Take the ones I've done and wash them, will you? I'm almost finished," she said and lifted the pot and handed it to Erin. She smiled at Dan as he lowered himself into the chair facing her. "We're freezing the beans I picked earlier," she explained, rapidly snapping the ends off the remaining beans.

"Can I help?" Dan asked, leaning toward her.

She looked up and smiled. "No, thanks. I really am almost done, and truthfully, I kind of enjoy doing this. It's one of those mindless activities that's very soothing. We just have to blanch the beans, then cool them and pack them in freezer bags. Erin and Eric are in charge of that part of the operation."

"What does 'blanch' mean in food speak?" he asked

idly. He wasn't really interested in her answer. He just liked to hear her voice out here in the darkness. He found that more soothing than snapping beans could ever be, he thought.

"It means to heat them quickly and briefly to stop metabolic action so they don't continue to age," she said. "Here, Erin," she called. "They're all done."

Dan got up and reached for the basket in her lap. "I'll take this inside," he said, turning toward the lighted kitchen. Erin was running water over the piles of beans in the sink and took the basket from his hand and dumped the contents into the sink. She deftly scooped piles of beans out of the water and into a perforated metal pot, then lifted the pot to fit inside another already on the stove. The lid was put in place and she glanced at the clock. "Just a couple of minutes in there and then they get cooled," she explained to Dan as she set a timer.

Eric moved to the sink carrying a bag of ice and a big plastic pan. "Hey, Dan, I hope you like beans. Lydia picked enough already this summer to fill the freezer," he said as he dumped the ice into the pan and turned on the water.

"Time's up, Eric. Move out of the way so you don't get burned," Erin said, nudging him with her elbow.

Erin lifted the inside pot and watched the water drain back into the kettle before upending the pot into the ice water.

"Anything I can do?" Dan asked. "This is a little out of my area of expertise, but I'm willing."

"Yeah," Erin answered. "Grab some iced tea and take it out to the porch while we finish up this mess." She turned to Eric. "Bring the freezer bags, will you? You labeled them, didn't you?"

They both ignored Dan so he took the iced tea pitcher from the refrigerator and carried it out to the porch and set it down next to a stack of plastic cups. "Those two are a very efficient team, aren't they?" he said to Lydia.

She murmured a sound of agreement and he turned to look closely at her in the dim light. Her eyes were closed and she sounded half-asleep. "Why don't you go to bed?" he asked quietly.

"Just taking a power nap," she said, opening her eyes. She smiled at him as he sat next to her and lifted his arm behind her to rest it along the back of the settee.

She closed her eyes again and Dan sat quietly, resisting the urge to touch her hair, to trail a finger along the side of her neck.

"I'm not really asleep, you know, just resting my eyes, saving my energy to take on the twins at Trivial Pursuit. They've won every time we've played this summer. I'm claiming you for my team tonight, okay?" she asked, still with her eyes closed.

"Do you play often?"

"Too often, I think," she replied. "Sometimes, we don't keep score, just read the questions and anybody answers. I tell myself it's educational." She laughed softly.

"I haven't played in years but I'm willing, as long as you don't hold me responsible for messing up their education," he said, smiling.

It was quiet on the porch for a few minutes and then Lydia asked, "How's the investigation going?" Her voice was pitched so low that he had to lean toward her to hear.

He spoke just as quietly. "Can't go there, Lydia."

She turned her head toward him and he could see that her eyes were open and she stared at him. "Okay. Can you talk about yourself?"

"Maybe." He smiled, letting his hand drift downward until it rested against her hair.

"Have you ever been hurt on the job?" Before he could answer, she went on, "Never mind. I don't need to know. That was just rampant nosiness."

He laughed. "I don't mind, and yes, I broke my ankle once chasing some dirtbag through the woods."

"Did you nail the bugger?"

"Yeah. It happened just as I tackled the guy and my partner was two seconds behind me."

He felt her hand on his knee and covered it with his own and grinned. "The worst part was being in a cast for six weeks. I admit I was not a good patient. I was twenty-five years old and raring to go. Now," he admitted, "I'd probably relax and let somebody take care of me." He raised an eyebrow at her and he swore he saw color rise up her neck to her face.

She pulled her hand out from under his and said, "Who would want to take on that job? You'd better not get hurt again until you figure that out."

"You could volunteer. I'd like that," he murmured, pitching his voice so she could just hear him as she stood up and reached for the pitcher on the table.

"Here," she said, handing him a full glass. "You need something to cool off? It's getting kind of hot out here."

He laughed out loud but didn't answer. Erin came onto the porch at that moment, flipping on the overhead light as she came through the door. Eric was right behind her, carrying a plate stacked high with brownies in one hand and the Trivial Pursuit box in the other.

Chapter Six

The dirt road was easy to follow as it cut across the farm toward the woods along the eastern edge. Dan had walked this route several times in the daylight and didn't really need the little bit of light provided by the waning moon overhead. He was jogging, carrying his pack, and dressed head to toe in black. He had a balaclava pulled over his head and only his eyes were visible. His head gear met the turtleneck of his shirt, providing night camouflage, with no skin showing, but also, he reflected, gave the mosquitoes no place to attack. A black vest was snapped closed at his chest and its pockets bulged with gear. His Glock was holstered under his left arm and assessable through a gap in the opening of the vest. It was 1:50 A.M. and except for the occasional sound of an animal scurrying away from him, it was quiet.

Kevin was crouched at the base of a huge oak and Dan squatted next to him, backed up against the trunk of the tree. He gave Kevin a thumbs-up and watched as he moved away and almost instantly disappeared, hidden by the underbrush and the trunks of the trees.

Dan turned and pulled himself up the side of the trunk, using the makeshift ladder formed by pieces of two-by-four lumber nailed to the tree. The platform was twenty feet above the ground and gave an unobstructed view of the logging road leading to the shack as well as the shack itself.

Lydia had pointed out this tree stand when they were walking back to the quad the other day. Well, walking and kissing, he grinned to himself. She had been a willing participant, he recalled, in his attempt to establish an innocuous scenario to explain why they were in the area. She had told him that there were several tree stands scattered through these woods because it was a popular deer hunting area. The platform was below the full canopy of branches, but high enough to be mostly invisible from the ground. Whoever had built it had done it to get an unobstructed view to the south, which placed it directly in line with the hunting shack they were watching. It was big enough to hold two people comfortably, if one could consider rough-cut wood twenty feet in the air comfortable, Dan thought.

He settled on the platform, his back against the tree,

and opened his pack. The night-vision goggles went on and covered the little bit of skin left uncovered by his head gear. His hands were protected by thin, black gloves. He couldn't use insect repellent because of the smell. To their regret, agents had learned that even the smell of old smoke on a smoker was detectable from a distance.

This was the dark of the night, the longest hours of a day, the hours when people were the least alert, and also the time when anyone who didn't want to have their business noticed would be out and about. Dan had been a part of many stakeouts and knew that the trick to staying alert was to keep his brain busy. He had used these hours to plan scenarios for his books and write them in his head. He was able to let his mind wander in any direction without losing the ability to detect any change in the area he was scanning. It was certainly a useful skill, he thought, since, otherwise, these night-time surveillance gigs could leave him practically comatose with boredom.

He was glad that he had stuffed a foam pad into his pack and he settled it under him now. The floor of this stand was made of splintery lumber, not the most comfortable surface for a long stay.

The woods were quiet. He could hear the air moving through the leaves, barely making them move. An occasional rustling in the duff under the trees told him that the little night creatures were busy. A shadow moving purposely toward his tree proved to be a coyote on the hunt. Out of the corner of his eye, he saw another silent shadow moving parallel with the first. The hunting partner was keeping pace. A half hour later he heard the bark of a coyote in the distance and an answering bark to the north. It was followed by the yipping of coyote pups, probably being taught to hunt, he thought.

There was plenty of small game out here. He thought he remembered reading that coyotes also ate fruit and berries. They were opportunists and concentrated on the easy kill. He hoped that didn't include Lydia's sheep. It was easy to see how, hunting in pairs, one coyote could distract a mother while the other one made the snatch and kill. Sheep didn't appear to have any defenses against a predator like that. A mother with twin lambs could be trying to protect one and leave the other vulnerable to attack. No doubt the coyotes used this to their advantage.

The airport was quiet. He could see the signal lights flashing, but he didn't expect any activity from that direction.

His butt was numb by 5 A.M. but he couldn't do anything about it except to shift his weight from side to side. Standing up was not an option, since the motion would be detectable by anyone watching. He was thinking about Chapter 9 when he saw a figure come out of the woods in front of the shack. He was clearly visible through the night-vision goggles. His shirt was tattered around the sleeves, the jeans were worn and the face was covered by a scraggly gray beard. He entered the building and came back out within seconds. He looked around and then walked back into the trees and disappeared from Dan's view.

Dan breathed slowly and shallowly, well aware that his position could be given away by the sound of the air rushing in and out of his lungs. The eastern sky was starting to lighten and he figured it was now or never for the pickup. Dawn would make it too easy to notice a stranger coming out of these woods or a vehicle driving out from the logging road. In a farming area like this, people were out early. The dairy farms did the morning milking at this hour and the milk truck went by on the highway at 6 A.M.

The birds had started making a racket a half hour earlier and Dan had just about given up hope for a pickup this morning when he suddenly became aware that the woods had become completely silent. The faint sound of a car engine could be heard breaking the silence. A black SUV glided slowly along the dirt track and stopped one hundred feet from the shack. The figure that emerged from the passenger side moved slowly, glancing around as he approached the shack entrance. Dan could see the gun in his right hand and turned his binoculars on the car. The tinted windows didn't allow him to see the driver but he had a clear view of the license plate at the rear. He saw the passenger come out of the shack, sliding a package into his left jacket pocket, and then move quickly back to the car. As soon as he was inside, the driver backed in a circle and retraced his path, moving slowly. The engine made very little sound and within seconds, Dan couldn't hear it.

Another ten minutes passed before he heard the twittering of the birds again. The eastern sky was definitely bright now although the sun wasn't visible yet.

There was more activity below him, squirrels mostly. A flock of wild turkeys marched by. There was no movement around the shack except for a squirrel jumping from a tree and landing on the roof. He sat on his haunches, looked around, and then took off along the edge of the roof and leaped to the ground. He headed straight for a tall oak at the edge of the little clearing and had run up it and disappeared in the canopy of leaves in the blink of an eye.

It was 6 A.M. and time to end this night's work, he thought. And hot damn, he had a description of the pickup vehicle and the license plate number. The drop-off guy definitely looked like a local and it wouldn't be too hard to ID him. Dan would bet that guy was a very minor player in this operation. The two in the SUV were most likely higher up the chain, but not at the top. Getting the top people was a priority, but to get to them, they had to gather up the lower-level tools at the same time. Right now, he and Kevin were in charge of getting this piece of the group ID'd and their modus operandi established while other agents were doing the same in other locations.

The day was rapidly brightening and Dan removed the night-vision goggles and repacked his pack. He had swung onto the makeshift ladder and was almost to the ground when he felt the hair on the back of his neck prickle. He dropped to the ground in a crouch and had the Glock in his hand before he realized that the coyotes had returned. The larger of the two stopped and stared at him. After an unblinking look, he continued on his way.

Dan huffed out his breath and laughed silently. Moving as silently as the coyotes, Dan slipped through the trees, keeping himself in the shadows. He couldn't be absolutely sure he was alone out here. He made a big circle, weaving through the trees, changing direction several times. Finally convinced that no one was watching him, he circled back to the farm road and jogged toward the cottage. The sound of a tractor could be heard in the distance, coming from the direction of Irv's dairy farm. The morning milking must be over by now, he thought. Later today he'd take a ride up there. But first he needed a shower and some sleep.

A few minutes later he was calling in the information, including the license plate number, so a trace could be put on it. With luck, it wouldn't turn out to be stolen.

The drop-off guy was the next problem. Kevin was already getting a fix on all the local farm employees as well as everyone connected with the airport. With the physical description he provided, the search could be narrowed down very quickly. Their instructions were to find and identify the guy but not to make any move to intercept. The higher-ups wanted this coordinated so they could move in on all the principals at the same moment. Scaring off anybody was not something that should happen. They wanted everyone caught in the net, no matter how unimportant they seemed.

A shower and shave helped but what he needed more was some sleep. The day was setting up to be hot, but the cottage stayed fairly cool, standing as it did in the shade of a grove of locust trees. He thought about eating for about two seconds and then lay down on top of the bed, wearing only boxers. He would sleep for a few hours, he thought, and then would check out some of the locals.

That thought had barely entered his mind when he fell asleep. Hours later, he awoke to the sound of a quad engine outside the cottage. He rolled off the bed and pulled on a pair of shorts before going to the door. Erin and Eric were just dismounting from their machine. As Dan stepped out onto the porch in his bare feet, Eric looked up and raised a hand in greeting.

"Hey, you want to come out on the boat with us this afternoon?" Eric asked. "It's so hot today and Lydia decided we needed a break. I think she's setting us up so we won't complain too much when we have to harvest the garlic and spend all day cleaning it."

Erin poked her brother with her elbow. "We won't be leaving until four o'clock and we bring food with us so we can stay out on the river 'til dark," she said, smiling at Dan. "We can swim from the boat so wear a bathing suit," she added.

Dan grinned at them. "Sounds like a great afternoon," he agreed.

"Come up to the house at four o'clock, then," Erin said. "We trailer the boat over there and launch it at Ferrytown. We're going to do the chores early so we can stay out late," she added.

"I'll be there," Dan said as the pair hopped on the quad, revved up the engine, and roared off with a wave in his direction.

Going back inside, he put together a couple of thick cheese sandwiches slathered with mustard and, with them on a plate in one hand and a glass of milk in the other, went back outside and sat on the swing to eat. He called Kevin on his cell phone and told him he was heading over to Irv's farm and then would be on the river for a while. Kevin grunted in reply and they agreed that there was no need to sit in a tree all night tonight.

"My backside has blisters from last night," Kevin groused. "I forgot how hard that wood can be after a while."

Dan laughed. "Too many cushy jobs lately, huh?"

"I wish," he said. "Call me at three and tell me what you find this afternoon and we can check in again at midnight. Think you'll be back from your date by then?"

"Not a date, Kev." *Although I wouldn't mind if it was,* Dan admitted to himself as he hung up.

After pulling a T-shirt over his head and sticking his feet into sneakers, he picked up his keys and went out to the car. Ten minutes later he was driving along a rutted dirt track leading toward the complex of farm buildings making up the dairy and milking parlor. It was absolutely quiet. He stopped and sat for a couple of minutes but no one appeared. He tried blowing the horn. Nothing. He needed to get a close-up look at the employees there, but it didn't look like that was going to happen that afternoon. He could hear the sound of a tractor rumbling in the distance and a mechanical *ka-thunk* that sounded every ten seconds or so.

The barns appeared to be empty of cows and people. It was three o'clock in the afternoon. Was everybody out on the river for the day, he wondered? The only things moving were a couple of kittens skittering around the corner of the barn, then turning and running back the way they had come.

He got back in his car and slowly backed around and headed out the dirt lane. At the end of the lane, he turned left and followed the narrow black-topped road toward the sound of the tractor. Somebody was making hay and the *ka-thunk*-ing sound was the baler as it kicked a bale from the back of the machine into a trailing wagon. He was too far away to see the driver of the tractor and the man's head was turned away from him, watching the machinery behind him. A little farther on, another tractor trundled along the field, pulling a rake that gathered the hay and laid it out in fluffy windrows. This was not his man, Dan thought. This one was clean shaven and had a pipe clenched in his teeth and the shiny dome of his skull glinted in the bright light. He looked bigger than the man he had seen this morning.

By now, Kevin should have been able to get some names and information on all the farm workers in the area. That should help him narrow things down so they didn't have to go searching out every farm in the county. A glance at the car clock got him moving faster, but not fast enough to bring him to the notice of the two men in the field. He was due to check in with Kevin in ten minutes. After that, if nothing turned up that required his attention, he planned on spending the rest of the day in a boat on the river.

Chapter Seven

Kevin answered on the first ring. "You're one minute late, Sonny," he greeted Dan. "I'm a very busy man, you know."

"Yeah, I'm impressed," Dan retorted. "Now, spill what you know."

According to Kevin's contact, there were three men working at Irv's dairy. A neighboring beef farm employed two college kids for the summer and a dairy farm three miles south was owned and run by two sisters, with no hired help. The airport was maintained by the brother of the owner, an elderly, mostly deaf amputee who walked with a cane. That about covered the local operations, according to Kevin. He would investigate further if they didn't turn up the man they were looking for in the immediate group. They would concentrate on Irv's three employees, two of whom Dan had seen that afternoon. He gave a brief description of each and learned their names. Scruffy was Billy Denzel who did the field work. Bald Head was Robert Carton, the dairy man, in charge of the milking parlor. The third man was Fred Johnson, the general help. Kevin described him as a heavy smoker with serious emphysema and a chronic cough.

It looked like they only had to check out one of the trio, the other two eliminated by their physical descriptions. Kevin planned to play lost tourist later that afternoon and drop by the farm to see if he could find all three. He had received driver's license photos of all of them by fax and planned to get up close and personal if he could, digital camera in hand. He emphatically vetoed the idea of Dan's accompanying him. No sense compromising his cover, he said.

Dan gave him his cell phone number again and told him that he would be out on the river.

"Don't worry. I won't call you," Kevin told him. "Next time I want to go hustling a pretty girl, you owe me."

Dan laughed, hung up, and quickly changed his jeans for a bathing suit and pulled a pair of nylon running pants over it. He tucked a windbreaker into a small duffel bag, along with his cell phone and sunglasses and sunscreen. After a quick look around the inside of the cottage, he went out the door, letting the screen slap closed behind him. He had done plenty of sailing on the Chesapeake Bay but had never been on a river of this magnitude. Eric had told him that they kept a twenty-foot cuddy cabin, powered by a five-liter V8 Chevrolet engine. That would be different too. His experience was with sail power.

A couple of minutes later he was knocking on the screened porch door and stepping inside at Lydia's invitation. He found her in the kitchen, spreading out a series of bread slices. "Here," she said, smiling in greeting, "put jam on half of these pieces of bread, will you? Erin and Eric will be back in a minute. They're doing the evening chores and I'm running behind."

She handed him a jar of strawberry jam and a big spoon and then picked up a flat-bladed spatula and stuck it into an open jar of peanut butter. "This happens to be everybody's favorite food when we go out on the boat," she told him. She glanced up at his face. "You're not allergic to peanuts, are you?"

He grinned. "No. This is a personal favorite of mine. Making excellent PB&J sandwiches is one of the few culinary accomplishments I can lay claim to," he added.

"Good. Finish these up and put them in those sandwich bags," she said, pointing to an open box of plastic bags next to the sink. "I need to get the cooler packed." She was at the refrigerator, pulling out two six-packs of soda and a collection of water bottles when he heard the sound of a quad coming up to the back door.

Erin bounced in the kitchen door. "Everything is fine

out there. The rams are fed and we filled their water tank." She reached for the cooler. "Here, give me that, Lydia. I'll pack the drinks. The cookies are already in a container." She was dressed in shorts pulled over her bathing suit and her legs and back were tanned. "Hey, Dan. Lydia put you to work, huh?" She grinned at him.

"He offered, I think. Well, maybe not," she admitted. "I have to change. I'll be back in a minute," she said, handing the cooler to Erin. "Where's Eric?"

"Putting the quad away. He'll be right here," Erin answered. "Go, will you?"

"Gone." Lydia laughed.

"Here, Dan. Put the sandwiches in here on top of the soda. I'll get some freezer packs," Erin said, handing him the cooler. He stacked the pile of sandwiches in the top of the cooler and made room for the freezer packs Erin retrieved from the freezer. They stuck the top in place and grinned at each other.

"Okay, I'm ready," Lydia said, coming back into the kitchen. She had changed into a shirt and shorts and Dan could see the top of her bathing suit through the thin cotton of her top. "The trailer is already hitched up, so grab the food, will you? And don't forget a sweatshirt or something for later. We may stay out 'til after dark if conditions are right," she added as she headed out the door.

She turned back. "Is that okay with you, Dan?"

"Yes, definitely. I've given myself the rest of the day off." He smiled at her and then grabbed the cooler

off the counter while Erin scooped up a canvas carryall from the table.

They were only ten minutes from the river, even trailering the boat. Lydia swung the SUV in a wide circle
and backed the trailer to an unloading ramp extending
into the water. With the back of the trailer half-
submerged, she set the parking brake and shut down
the engine. Erin and Eric spilled out the rear doors and
grabbed wheel chocks from the cargo area. Dan got out
to help but the twins had obviously gone through this
routine many times before and had the trailer and SUV
tires chocked before he got to the back of the vehicle.
Then Eric hopped up on the trailer while Erin pulled
the cooler and their duffel bags from the back of the
SUV and stowed them in the boat.

Dan reached to release the chains securing the boat
to the trailer and gave a thumbs-up to Eric when he had
completed a circuit of the boat. Eric released the winch
and slowly let the boat slide down the skids into the water. Erin was already standing up on the bow with a
rope coiled in her hands. She tossed it to Dan, indicating he should secure it to a piling at the side of the
ramp. This done, she hopped off into the shallow water
and unhooked the winch cable from the ring on the
front of the boat, tossing the cable onto the trailer.

Eric grabbed the chocks from behind the wheels of
the trailer and SUV and Dan bent to do the same on his
side. They tossed them in the back of the SUV, closed
the tailgate, and then Eric signaled to Lydia. She

slowly pulled away from the launch ramp and drove toward the parking area. She neatly lined up the trailer and backed into a parking spot, slid out of the SUV, and walked back toward them.

Dan moved to meet her and they both walked back toward the boat. "You have a well-trained crew, don't you?" he remarked.

"They've been doing this since they were pretty young. Coming here to their grandparents' for the summer gives my sister-in-law the opportunity to go back to Ireland to visit her parents. The kids are always anxious to come here, so it works out well. They've gone to Ireland for a few weeks several times, to visit their grandparents there, but they have a lot more freedom to do things they like here," she explained.

She waded into the water and Erin extended her hand to pull her up into the boat. Eric was ready to release the tie-up line, so Dan followed Lydia over the side onto the deck. While Eric released the line and threw it toward Erin, Lydia moved to the front of the boat. A turn of the key brought the engine to life and Eric pulled himself out of the water and into the boat. Erin pulled bright-orange flotation vests from their storage place in the little cabin and Lydia waited until they had donned them before backing the boat away from the launching ramp and then turning it toward the vast expanse of water beyond the cove.

There was a light breeze out on the river, enough to keep them cool. Only a few wispy clouds were visible to the west and the sun glinted on the water. From his seat on the side bench, Dan could see gulls wheeling overhead, their raucous cries echoing over the water. The birds had followed the ships and barges coming upriver from the ocean ninety miles away.

He lounged back against the side, sticking his legs out in front of him, his arms resting on the side rails. It had been months since Dan had been out on the water and he leaned his head back and relaxed, enjoying the flow of air generated by their forward motion.

There was plenty of other traffic on the river. Sailboats tacked back and forth, speed boats threw up trails of spray, some of them pulling water-skiers. The sound of Jet Skis came from farther to the west on the river, and there were a couple of small boats stationary in the water. Even with all that activity, it was peaceful, and Dan could feel himself getting drowsy.

Before he fell completely asleep, he kicked off his sneakers and sat up and pulled his running pants off. The twins were already stripped down to their bathing suits and Lydia had pulled her T-shirt off but was still wearing shorts over her bathing suit.

Lydia slowed their forward motion and called to Erin to get some sunscreen on herself and her brother before they went in the water. Erin flipped the plastic bottle to Dan when she was done and then she and her brother dived off the side into the water. The engine was shut down now and Dan perceived the drift caused by the current.

He slathered some sunscreen over his chest and arms and legs, knowing how easy it was to get a serious burn out on the river, from the sun combined with the glare off the water. He stood up and moved toward Lydia, still seated by the wheel. He handed her the bottle and watched as she spread a layer on her face and neck and chest. She was already tanned, and as she bent forward to reach her legs, Dan could see the pale skin under the top edge of her bathing suit.

Lydia turned toward him with a smile. "Let me put some on your back. You can't reach it, can you?"

He turned his back to her and enjoyed the sensation of her hand smoothing the lotion over his skin. For a woman who did a lot of manual labor, her hand was remarkably soft.

Lydia moved her hand briskly over his back and the top of his shoulders. "I'm trying not to miss any spots," she said before she lightly slapped his back with the flat of her hand. "All done." She handed him the bottle as he turned toward her and then presented her back to him.

Dan shook his head as he squeezed some sunscreen onto his hand. He was going to have to get in the water and cool off before he did something he shouldn't. Smoothing lotion all over her back was enough to leave him weak in the knees, he thought. He ran his hands up the sides of her neck, rubbing the skin gently and lingering for a second on the lobe of her ear.

Lydia was very still. Then she drew in a big breath and took a step away from him. "Thanks," she said and went to stand at the wheel.

Dan flipped over the side of the boat and went into the water. At least she hadn't turned around and smacked him, he thought.

The water was cool and there was enough of a current to make swimming against it a challenge. He turned onto his back and floated, squinting up at the cloudless sky. He heard the twins splashing each other and briefly tuned them out. He was feeling pretty mellow. Lydia had not pushed him away. He hadn't been able to resist touching her more than he should have. Putting sunscreen on her back had not been an invitation to seduction, he was pretty sure. But he knew she was aware of him in more than a casual way. And certainly he was aware of her.

He turned over and started away from the boat, swimming with an easy crawl for a hundred yards and then retraced his path back toward the boat. He was once again floating on his back, glancing at some clouds that had started to build to the west, when Eric swam close and flipped onto his back. He saw Erin swim to the side of the boat and pull herself over the side. Lydia turned to her as Erin said something and he saw Lydia shake her head and look over toward him. He grinned back at her.

Eric turned his head to look at him. "Are you married?"

Dan flashed a quick look at Eric, floating next to him, staring at the sky.

"No, I'm not, Eric. I never had much interest in it before," he admitted.

"Well, just asking, you know. We could see you and Lydia from here. I'm going back to the boat. It's time to eat," he said as he swam away.

Well, that was interesting, Dan thought. The twins were very observant and very protective of their aunt. He had thought that his interest in Lydia was pretty well hidden, but obviously not.

Dan stayed in the water for another few minutes before swimming to the side of the boat. Erin reached over to help him up and handed him a towel. "Thanks," he said. As he rubbed at his hair, he looked at her and smiled. "You have no need to be wary of me, Erin," he murmured. "I'm not looking for just a fling with your aunt. I hope you'll trust me."

"My aunt is pretty naive for someone her age. Eric and I love her very much," she stated. "I happen to like you," she said. "Eric is being sort of macho, so don't screw up," she warned.

She turned away and he was left drying himself off, kind of amazed that his romantic inclinations were being scrutinized by a pair of fourteen-year-olds. He realized, though, that he had done the same thing when his sister was dating, passing comments on one or the other of her boyfriends. He wondered how she had tolerated him.

He looked up to see Lydia smiling at him, and moved forward until he stood shoulder to shoulder with her. Eric was pulling the cooler out of its storage place.

"They haven't scared you off, have they?" she asked, not looking at him.

"Nope, no way," he said, shifting slightly so that his shoulder touched hers,

"Good." She flashed him a smile and turned toward the cabin.

He watched her move away and let out his breath. "Good," she'd said. And it was very good, he thought.

The engine rumbled to life and the boat moved in a lazy circle before heading back up stream. He realized that they had drifted several miles from where they had entered the river and were a lot closer to the vehicle bridge spanning the river and connecting the east side to a much larger town on the west side. He knew that this was a tidal river and the tide must have been running out while they had been swimming. They had not dropped anchor, which meant that the boat had drifted with them, leaving the illusion that they were stationary in the water. He was aware that if Lydia had dropped anchor, the tide would have taken them downstream as they swam and left them far from the boat. He wondered how fast the tide ran here and turned to ask Eric.

"Three to four miles an hour, I think," he replied. "And the salt line is downriver about twenty miles. Lots of communities up this way tap the river for drinking water, but twenty miles downriver, it's too salty to use without desalinization." Eric was sitting on the bench, the cooler tucked between his feet, and Dan sat down next to him, leaning his back against the side rail.

"Do you water-ski on the river, Eric?" he asked.

"Sure. Lydia really likes to ski, so we come out here pretty often when there's someone else to drive the boat. They let me when we're just out cruising, but Grandpa doesn't think I'm ready to do it if I was pulling a skier." He shrugged. "He's probably right. He usually is," he admitted. "Can you ski?" he asked.

"Snow ski, yes, but I've never tried water-skiing. I'd like to," Dan admitted.

"I'll tell Lydia and the next time we come out, you can try it," Eric said with enthusiasm. "It's great fun."

They became aware that the engine was quiet. They were opposite the launching dock and Lydia had cut the engine. Eric got up and quickly moved over to his sister to help lower the anchor. When he came back to Dan, he lifted the cooler onto the bench and opened it.

Lydia had the duffel bag open and pulled several sweatshirts out, handing one to Erin as she came over and passing one to Eric. She raised an eyebrow at Dan and held up another shirt. He shook his head and reached for his windbreaker, stuffed in the bottom of his bag. The wind had picked up slightly, and although the sun was still pretty high in the sky, it seemed a lot cooler than it had been.

Lydia sat down on the bench next to him and pulled

a sweatshirt over her head. Dan reached behind her to pull the hem into place at her waist and she moved back, holding his hand in place against her back. He spread his fingers out to curve around her waist and she didn't withdraw. He left his hand there until Eric handed him a sandwich and Erin tossed a can of soda at him at the same time. He grinned at both of them and Lydia laughed.

"I love eating peanut butter sandwiches out on the river." Erin sighed. She lay back on the deck with her eyes closed. "I wish we could stay out here all the time."

Eric sat beside her Indian-style, chugging his soda. "Nah. You'd hate it after about three days. There aren't any books out here," he said. "Besides, I'd miss riding the quad if all we ever did was cruise the river. And," he added, "you wouldn't like it out here during a thunderstorm."

He pointed toward the west where black clouds had started to gather. Lydia turned in that direction, stood up quickly, and said, "We're out of here. Get the anchor, kids!"

As she spoke, the wind started to pick up and the water started to get choppy. It was a fast-moving storm, Dan realized, and reached to help get the anchor out of the water. The engine roared to life and the boat started to move as soon as Eric shouted an "All clear." They all hurried to don the life jackets while Lydia turned the boat toward the dock.

It only took a couple of minutes to get into the cove and glide up to the dock but already there were white-caps showing on the river and the wind had strength-ened enough that the flag hanging from its pole next to the dock stood straight out. Eric and Dan jumped off onto the dock and secured the boat while Lydia shut down. Erin had collected their gear and handed it off to Eric before jumping down. Lydia followed her and then jogged toward the SUV. She drove toward the dock and maneuvered around, lining the trailer up with the ramp with no hesitation, and backed the trailer down the ramp and into the water.

Eric grabbed the winch cable and attached it to the boat, and Dan quickly released the rope securing the boat to the dock. The boat slid up the rails of the trailer and settled in place. Lightning flashed and thunder boomed almost overhead as Lydia pulled forward. Erin was already attaching the side tie-downs, securing the boat. The rain came down suddenly, drenching them in an instant. Dan grabbed the cooler and duffel bags and threw them in the back of the SUV before getting in the front seat. Erin and Eric piled in the back and Lydia pulled farther into the parking area, leaving the dock and ramp clear.

She looked over her shoulder and laughed as the twins performed identical shakes to rid their faces of some of the water running down from their hair. "Grab a towel from the back, will you? Dan needs some help here too," she said, grinning at him. His shirt was soaked through, showing his broad shoulders, and his hair hung in his eyes, with water dripping off his nose.

"You think it's funny, huh?" he asked her and reached over and grabbed her, holding her against his chest and letting the water running off his hair soak her neck. She squirmed against him, trying to lean away from him.

"Enough, enough! I'm not laughing anymore," she exclaimed.

Erin tossed a towel over into the front and he used it to wipe his face and rub his hair. He looked over at Lydia and grinned. She was laughing at him and reached over to smooth his hair down. Her eyes locked on his and her hand stilled for a second. She shivered despite the fact that she wasn't the one sitting there in soaking-wet clothes. She pulled her hand away and gripped the steering wheel as she felt a flush rise up her face. She was not going to fall in love with a man who moved from place to place with his job, a job that placed him in danger! She was a farmer, tied to the land, a scientist who planned to spend her life studying the same patch of ground where she was born. They were incompatible!

Erin leaned forward and said, "The storm's moving on, Lydia. Let's get home so we can change, okay?"

"Uh, sure, Erin," Lydia managed before she put the SUV in gear and drove out of the parking area.

"Eric said you like to water-ski. Would you teach me?" Dan asked.

His casual question brought her back to reality and she glanced over to see him looking straight ahead, watching the wet road ahead of them. The sky was already clearing and the sun was glinting off the puddles and the water dripping from the trees.

"Will you be around that long?" she asked.

"I'd like to stay around here and explore things," Dan answered. "You could probably help me."

Lydia looked at him briefly before turning her attention back to the road. "Yes," she told him, a little smile curving her lips. "That could be fun. I haven't visited the tourist spots since I was a child."

"Yeah, that too," he said, sending her a quick grin.

Lydia pulled into the driveway leading to the machinery shed before she could reply, and instead concentrated on backing the trailer under cover. Eric got out to set the jack in place and unhitch the trailer and then climbed back inside. "All set," he said to Lydia and she pulled away and drove back to the road and entered the driveway leading to the farmhouse.

When she had parked under a big maple tree by the back door, Dan reached over and touched her arm. "I'll see you tomorrow. I need to get cleaned up and I have some phone calls to make. Thanks for a great time." He climbed out at the same time the twins piled out. After retrieving his duffel bag from the back, he wished them a good night and started down the path to the cottage.

"See you tomorrow, Dan," Erin called to his retreating figure and he lifted a hand in a wave before slinging the duffel over his shoulder.

Lydia slid out of the SUV and saw Erin grinning at her. "Did he kiss you yet?"

Lydia raised her eyebrows, frowning slightly. "Of course not."

"Well, he wants to," Erin said emphatically, running up the steps to the porch and following her brother inside.

Lydia grabbed the cooler and carryall from the back of the SUV and carried them into the kitchen. She could hear the downstairs shower running and assumed the upstairs one would also be in use. She had remained dry, having the good fortune to be in the SUV when the rain had started, and she just needed to change out of her bathing suit. Dan's attempt to get her wet had left her shirt a little damp but it was already drying. His playfulness was a pleasant surprise. The last guy she had dated seriously had been kind of stiff and didn't like to touch casually the way Dan did.

Not that she was dating Dan, but she admitted to herself that he was pleasant to be around and she liked him. Her dad and mom would like him too, she thought. Erin was treating him like an older brother and Eric was comfortable with him. His job could be dangerous at times, if her suspicions about what he did were true. He hadn't talked about it but she had noticed a long, ragged scar on the back side of his left shoulder. It certainly could have been put there by a bullet, but just as likely could have a dozen other origins. Really, she thought, he could have fallen out of a tree when he was a kid, or taken a header off his bike, or caught it on a fence. She wondered if he would tell her the truth if she asked him. Probably not.

The phone rang once and stopped. A minute later Eric called down from upstairs to tell her to pick it up. Her parents were calling from California. Her father actually raved about the Alaskan cruise. It had been hard to imagine her father away from the farm for more than a few days, let alone a few weeks.

"Everything is fine here, Dad. The calves look good." She listened a minute and then assured him that they weren't having any problems with the coyotes, although they carried a gun on their rounds of the animals. "By the way, there's a guy renting the cottage for a month. I didn't think you'd mind. He said he knew Uncle Mark." She listened for a minute. "I checked with Uncle Mark. He seemed to know him. Personally I think he's DEA, but Uncle Mark wouldn't say anything."

When her mother got on the phone, she sounded really excited. "It's so beautiful. You really should see it, Lydia," she enthused. "Did your Dad say someone is staying in the cottage? Who is it?"

"Just a guy looking for a place to stay while he finishes a book, Mom. You'd like him. He went out on the boat with us this afternoon." She listened for a minute. "Yeah, early thirties, I guess." Then, "No, he doesn't wear a wedding ring. Stop, Mom! What else have you done on this trip? We really miss you and Dad. When are you coming home, anyway?" she asked.

She listened for another minute, then said, "Mom, really, he's just a nice guy who's only here for a few weeks." She listened again and then said, "Bye, we love you both."

Chapter Eight

"Hey, Kev. What's up?" Dan stretched out on the bed, cradling the receiver against his shoulder.

"Got some more information on our three guys. You'll love some of this."

"Okay. Give it to me." Dan stood and went to the dresser. He grabbed a pad of paper and pen and went back to the bed, stretching out again, as Kevin laughed.

"Sounds like you're passed out on the bed. She wearing you out?" he asked.

"Just give me the info, and try to keep your mind out of the gutter, buddy. She's a nice woman," Dan added, "with two kids acting as duennas."

"Too bad," Kevin laughed again. "Anyway, the three guys working for Irv are a collection of our finest citizens. Your guy, Billy, has worked there for over twenty years. He's forty-five, married with four kids. The kids have been taken away and placed in foster care several times. They claim to love the kids but neglect them."

"Like how?" Dan asked.

"Like spend his entire paycheck on a wreck of a car and forget to get food for the kids. Like borrow fifty dollars from the boss and he and the wife spend it all at the county fair and leave the kids home with no food."

"Nice." Dan commented.

"He's a working fool, out in all weather with no hat, jacket wide open, no gloves even when it's zero degrees and the wind is howling. Shows up for work but whines all the time."

"And?" Dan asked.

"There's more. The wife has a seventeen-year-old boyfriend and the thirteen-year-old daughter is pregnant. They all live in a two-bedroom trailer on the farm. They're getting maximum assistance from the state. Irv pays him the minimum allowed by law but provides the housing, such as it is. They steal milk, calves, piglets, hay, and gasoline, and anything else movable."

"They sound delightful," Dan said dryly. "I can hardly wait to meet him up close and personal."

"The other guy, Robert, the one you described with the pipe, went to work for Irv when he was eighteen and he's now forty-seven. He lives in an old tenant house up the road from the farm. That place is owned by an elderly lady who lives in a nursing home and Irv made a deal with her executors to let Robert occupy the tenant house in exchange for mowing the lawns and shoveling snow. The tenant house is a dump. There's trash all over the place. He's got cages of chickens and turkeys and ducks. There are a couple of pigs in a shed and everything is filthy. The local word is that he's downright mean. Got mad at a cow and shoved a pitchfork in her eye and blinded her. Supposed to be a worse thief than Billy. His wife stays in the house all day and watches TV and the two boys are into petty crime. So far," he added.

"Why would a farmer keep him on the place?" Dan wondered out loud. "What about number three?"

"Getting to him," Kevin said. "Robert's been arrested for petty theft, and beating Billy's wife when she wouldn't give him money that he said Billy owed him."

"Jeez, what a group. Is there anything redeeming about the third guy?"

Kevin grunted. "Fred is sixty-five, has worked for Irv for thirty-some years. He's got bad emphysema and still smokes. He can hardly walk, he's so short of breath. No criminal record. Lives in a trailer on the farm. Wife died three years ago. Daughter is Robert's wife."

"Well, we can eliminate him, I guess," Dan said. "The guy I saw didn't seem to be short of breath and sure didn't move like he had anything physically wrong with him."

"This guy, Billy, is my personal choice. He matches your physical description," Kevin added. "The boss says to tail him the next time we expect the plane, which is day after tomorrow."

"Yeah, good. Why don't you meet me at the bookstore in town, tomorrow at four. Bring the photos."

"Will do. See you then."

Dan hung up and stared up at the ceiling for a minute, thinking that this case could wind up pretty soon. He stood and headed for the shower.

He had just pulled a pair of sweats over his boxers when he heard the sound of a quad moving slowly up the driveway to the cottage. Its headlights cut across the porch as he moved to the door. The twins climbed off and Dan moved to the bedroom, grabbed a shirt, and pulled it over his head. He was tucking it into his pants as he went to the door and greeted Erin. Eric was behind her, carrying a cardboard carton.

"Hey, Dan. Lydia sent us over with some food. She thought you might still be hungry since supper on the boat got interrupted," she announced. Eric moved forward as he pushed open the screen to let them in.

"Mental telepathy." He laughed. "I was just thinking about finding something to eat."

Eric handed the box to him. "Thanks, Eric. And thank your aunt for me. You guys want some?"

"We already ate, but Erin added a big bag of chocolate chip cookies." Eric sounded hopeful. "You could eat out on the porch if the mosquitoes aren't too bad," Eric said. "We brought some punk sticks to burn so you could sit out there."

"Let's try it," he said, going out the door with the box in his hands. "Hey, Eric, there's one of those propane lighters in the kitchen drawer. Grab it and we'll try out these punk sticks."

Dan sat down on the swing and Erin leaned over the box and extracted a dozen thin, brown sticks, which she proceeded to jam into cracks in the railing around the porch and along the swing. Eric appeared with the lighter in his hand and Erin directed him to all the sticks she had planted. The light smoke and pungent smell reminded him of a summer Boy Scout camp where he had spent some time twenty years before.

He pulled the bag of cookies from the box and tossed it to Erin. "Why don't you call your aunt and ask her to come for dessert?" he suggested. "Phone is on the table," he said as she moved toward the cottage door.

"I don't know if she'll come. She was hunched over the computer screen and muttering when we left. She said she had to get all the new data on the strawberry plantings entered." She looked over her shoulder at him. "She was out really early this morning, driving over to the strawberry farm. They were doing the next set of measurements today."

Dan could hear the murmur of her voice as she spoke on the phone. She was back in a minute, smiling. "She's going to walk over. She said she's had more than enough of data entry for one day. Truthfully," she added, "it's not that hard to drag her away from the computer. She'd much rather be outside."

Eric passed her the cookie bag as she sat on the porch floor with her back against the railing. Dan ate the chicken salad sandwich and chips, enjoying the quiet and the view of the pond with the moon shining on it. There was enough light to see Lydia moving up the driveway a few minutes later, accompanied by her dog. When she climbed the stairs to the porch, the dog settled on the grass and put her head down. Dan smiled at Lydia and patted the seat next to him. After she sat down, he set the swing in motion with his foot. It was quiet except for the usual night sounds and the slight creak of the chain against the hook as the swing moved slowly, forward and back.

Lydia broke the silence after a few minutes. "You have the nicest view from up here. We don't really have any view up at the house," she said softly.

"I like it," Dan said. "Particularly on a night like this with the moon reflecting off the pond. It's kind of otherworldly." He pushed the swing into motion again. "Do you skate on it in the winter? It looks about the right size for a hockey game."

Lydia turned to look at him. "It's funny that you should ask that, because that's exactly what we did every time it froze thick enough to skate on. It's spring fed and about eight feet deep in the middle, and we've had times when one end of the pond would stay free of ice." She laughed softly. "My brother Rob dumped the garden tractor in it one winter. He had rigged a snow-plow to the front and was clearing the ice when he went through at the north end. Fortunately, he was close to shore and jumped off. The tractor went down but the water was shallow enough near the edge that it didn't sink completely. Rob and Dad brought in a big tractor with a bucket on the front over to the pond. Dad drove it up to the edge of the water and Rob dangled off the bucket to get a chain wrapped around the part of the plow sticking out of the water."

"I never heard this story," Eric said from his position on the floor.

Lydia laughed again. "Not one of your father's finer moments. Anyway," she continued, "he and Dad got that garden tractor out of the water and I know they thought the engine was done for because it had been underwater. They let it sit there while he and a couple of friends finished clearing the snow off the ice and when he went back to it, he cranked it over once and the thing started right up. He just stood there grinning like it was a miracle or something."

She sighed softly. "We sure had a lot of fun. We even had night games. We'd drag the generator and some work lights down there and skate under the lights. Somebody would show up with hot chocolate and coffee and food and it would turn into a party."

Dan reached over and linked his fingers with hers where her hand rested on her thigh. She didn't pull away but relaxed her hand in his. She had her head against the back of the swing and turned slightly so she could look at him. He smiled at her and lifted her hand over to his thigh, stroking the palm with his thumb.

He listened to the sounds of the night, relaxing against the back of the swing. A hoot owl could be heard from the other side of the pond. The frogs were making a racket and he could hear the faint sound of a dog barking in the distance. The cry of a red-tailed hawk echoed across the valley and Lydia's dog snuffled in her sleep. He couldn't remember the last time life had felt this peaceful. There was always another case, another adrenaline rush, in the life he lived. But he could easily get used to this, he thought, hearing a faint sigh and raising Lydia's hand to his lips for an instant.

"How's the strawberry data looking?" Dan asked, turning his head so he could see her.

"Excellent, thanks. I was over there by dawn this morning. The measuring is pretty tedious, but Ben and Suzanne have been a tremendous help. Suzanne and I went all through school together, from kindergarten up until college," Lydia explained. "By the way," she added, "I saw Billy Denzel walking out of the airport access road as I went by there at five-thirty or six this morning." She slanted a glance at him. "The seaplane came in last night, didn't it?"

He just looked at her and smiled. "Are you sure it was Billy Denzel?"

At her nod, he asked, "He works at the dairy farm across from the airport, doesn't he?"

"Yeah. Why are you interested in him?"

"No reason. I took a ride up around that way and saw some guys running machinery in the fields." She looked skeptical and he added, "Just curious about the natives."

"I've known him since I was a kid, Dan. What do you need to know about him?"

Eric and Erin were both stretched out flat on the porch floor, not moving. Dan played with her fingers, rubbing the pad of his thumb over her knuckles. She didn't pull her hand away and he rubbed his thumb slowly back and forth.

Lydia shivered slightly, despite the warmth of the night. The motion of his thumb felt intimate, even with all these chaperones. Lydia leaned toward him, bringing her shoulder closer to his. She kept her voice low, almost speaking in his ear. Now it was Dan's turn to shiver and he pulled gently on her arm, bringing her up against his side.

"Billy Denzel has always been very polite to me. Some vestige of gallantry in him, I guess. He's uneducated, sly, devious, and not above lying, cheating, and stealing. He's amoral and not someone you'd want your daughter to bring home. He smells to high heaven and so it's best to stay upwind of him." She giggled softly. "I've seen Irv driving down the road with his head stuck out the window when he has Billy in the truck with him. As far as I know, he's never done anything but farm work. The children have been placed in foster care a couple of times."

"Is he into drugs?" Dan asked.

She seemed to consider her answer before she said, "I've never seen anything to suggest he's a user. Dealing the stuff would be more his style." She shifted so she was looking directly at him, pulling her hand free. "He's not smart enough to think up something on his own, but he could be bought."

When he didn't comment, she asked, "Do you think he's involved in whatever is going down at the airport?"

"All I can tell you is that it was pretty crowded in the woods last night."

Eric stirred and rolled over, groaning. "These boards are too hard," he grumbled. "I've gotta go to bed. You coming, Erin?" he asked as he nudged her with his foot.

"Okay," she answered, climbing to her feet and following her brother down the steps. Flirt raised her head to watch but didn't move from her position on the grass,

"See you, Dan," they chorused as Eric started the engine and the quad slowly moved down the driveway.

"Did I thank you for sending dinner?" Dan asked Lydia.

"Such as it was," she grinned. "I'm going, too," she said, as she stood up.

"I'll walk you home," Dan murmured as he came to his feet.

"No need. Flirt will escort me home, but thanks, anyway," she said as she walked down the steps and then bent over to touch the dog gently on the top of her head. "Come on, Flirt. Time to go. See you, Dan," she called over her shoulder as she walked down the driveway.

Chapter Nine

It was hot. It was humid. It was July. And now it was raining. Eric grumbled all through breakfast while Erin just stared at him in disbelief.

"What is the matter with you, brother dear?"

"Nothing," he hissed. "Keep your voice down. I'm trying to convince Lydia that I need R & R today so she won't send us to the ram's barn to clean it out."

"She's not going to buy it. We were out on the boat just yesterday. And we're going to have to do it soon, you know. The bedding is almost up to the top of the grain feeders."

"Well, why don't you tell her you don't feel well or something?" he asked.

"Because I feel fine, Eric," she retorted.

Lydia came into the kitchen and walked behind

Eric's chair, slapping him on the top of the head with
the flat of her hand. "Stow it, buddy. I heard everything.
We'll all do it. It won't be so bad," she sympathized.
"The rams will be much more comfortable if we do it,
so go hitch the manure spreader to the tractor and pull
it up by the barn. Erin and I will be right there."

Erin grinned at her brother and watched him as he
stood up and then clutched his chest dramatically.
"Forget it, Eric. She's not buying any of it," she said.
"Nice try, though."

Eric shrugged his shoulders and walked out, starting to whistle as soon as he hit the driveway.

Lydia laughed and dumped dishes in the sink. "Are
you planning to make something with those strawberries I brought from Suzanne's yesterday?" she asked
"I have a real craving for waffles with strawberries
and vanilla ice cream for dinner."

"Yum. One of my favorites." Erin was loading the
dishwasher as she answered. "Will Dan be here for
dinner?"

"As far as I know."

"He's pretty nice, don't you think, Lydia?" Erin
glanced at her aunt. "What were you talking about last
night?"

"He was just asking about the local characters. He
saw a couple of Irv's men making hay the other day,
so I was just giving him background." She laughed.
"Maybe he'll put them in a book."

"You think?" Erin smiled, wiping her hands on a

dish towel. "I'm done here, Lydia. I'll go down and help Eric, okay?"

"Sure. I'll be there in a minute. I need to make a couple of phone calls."

Her uncle Mark wasn't much more forthcoming than the last time, when she called him at home and pressed him about her tenant's activities. He finally told her, flat out, to mind her own business. Lydia laughed. "You don't scare me, Uncle Mark. But don't worry, I won't try to interfere. I was just curious about what's really going on."

"Just don't get in the way, Lydia," he warned. After exchanging news with her aunt, Lydia hung up and sat at her desk for another minute. Without telling her anything, her uncle had confirmed her suspicion that Dan had something else on his agenda other than writing a book. Now that she was positive Dan was DEA, what difference did it make? she wondered.

Walking down the lane to the barns, with Flirt at her heels, she told herself to stop thinking about a man who would only be there for another couple of weeks, and concentrate on getting her dissertation finished. She was planning the garlic harvest in her head as she approached the rams' barn and heard the radio blaring. The manure spreader was overflowing and Eric was just mounting the seat of the tractor. It was still raining lightly as he pulled away with his load.

The twins had already cleaned most of the pen and

Erin leaned on her fork and grinned at Lydia. "Nice timing, Auntie."

"I try. And sometimes it just pays to be the boss," she retorted.

"I'll have to remember that when I grow up," Erin said, bending over to pick up a rake and then tossing it to Lydia. "Here, boss, rake out that part we already cleaned while I finish this section."

Lydia pulled the pickup truck into a space by the curb. Her destination was the bookstore, half a block away. The bed of the truck was filled with rolls of fence wire and bundles of metal fence posts that she had picked up at the farm supply store.

She patted the hood of the truck as she circled around in front of it. She had named it Big Blue when she had bought it five years earlier. It had been ridden hard and put away wet, her Dad had laughed, but it had four wheel drive and low mileage, and she had wanted it. The welder who lived down the road had applied a sheet of steel to the floor of the bed to cover the rusted out spots. Lydia had ground down the rusted places on the body, primed them and painted them, and Big Blue was ready to go.

She admitted it didn't get great gas mileage but it had turned out to be a very useful workhorse around the farm. Besides, it gave her a certain cachet among the academics when she drove it around the university.

She hopped up the two steps leading to the entrance of the bookstore, pulled open the door, and greeted her friend Sophie, who was leaning against the front counter, the phone caught between her ear and shoulder.

"Hey, Lydia. You're here for that book you ordered," she stated. "Hold on a minute."

Lydia wandered toward the back of the store while she waited. She had reached the end of a row of shelving housing paperback mysteries when she saw Dan standing with his back to her. She saw the blond-haired man sitting in an armchair look up and speak to him and Dan slowly and casually stepped away and then turned toward her. He was dressed in running shorts and wore a T-shirt wet with sweat. It clung to his chest and strained at his biceps. The shorts were nylon and outlined his body very nicely. She admired his well-muscled legs before bringing her gaze back to his face. He was grinning at her, completely relaxed and at ease.

Which was more than she could say about herself, she thought. Her ratty jeans and worn T-shirt, while comfortable, were not a fashion statement, but Dan didn't seem to notice. He was looking into her eyes, holding her in place with a warm look.

She noticed that the guy in the chair was pretending to read, but she saw his eyes flick from Dan to her and back again. Dan walked toward her, his running shoes making a slight squeak on the tile floor.

"Hey, you caught me visiting my favorite store in this town," he said, touching her arm. It was obvious to Lydia that he wanted her to be distracted from his contact with Blond Hair, but Lydia recognized him as the same man standing outside the hardware store the first time Dan had come into the village with them, and the same man who had stared at Sophie through the store window before he winked at her and strolled away. The man was a stranger and didn't look like a tourist and she was convinced there was a connection between the two men.

"Sophie called to tell me to come pick up a book I had on order. You've met her, haven't you? She owns this place," she said as she walked back to the front counter and leaned her elbows on its high surface. She looked at Sophie, who was smiling at her. Dan extended his hand to her as Lydia made the introductions. He congratulated Sophie on the store and then told Lydia he was finished here and would see her back at the farm.

"Hang on, Dan. It's too hot to be running. The truck is outside. I can give you a ride, if you'll wait just a minute. I have to pay for this," she said, pulling a credit card out of the pocket of her T-shirt and handing it to Sophie.

When she went out the front door of the store a few minutes later, a book tucked under her arm, she found Dan standing on the sidewalk, waiting, and she cocked her head in the direction of the truck and started walking toward it.

She climbed into the driver's seat, turned the key, and reached over to crank the air-conditioning to the max, waiting for the cool air to dissipate some of the heat built up in the cab.

"Are you going to tell me who that guy is, or not?"

"Or not," he replied, flashing a grin in her direction.

"Careful. You could still run back to the farm," she growled.

"That would be cruel. I took the long way around to the village and I really wasn't looking forward to adding three more miles to the ten I already did. But you're right," Dan added, "it's too hot at this time of day and the humidity is too high to make this fun."

"I've never seen the fun in it, anyway," Lydia said. "And don't think I've forgotten your buddy in the bookstore. He's the same one who went in the hardware store ahead of you the day you arrived, right?"

"Must have been a coincidence." He shrugged.

"Right. Like I believe in coincidence."

Dan ignored her last comment and asked what she was doing in town. She knew what he was doing—distracting her—but she let him do it anyway. She dropped him off at the driveway to the cottage and pulled up alongside the machinery shed. Eric came out of the shed just as she stopped the truck and, together, they got the rolls of wire out of the truck and stored them under cover.

"What's going on, Eric?" she asked, noticing an oil smear on his forearm.

"I just changed the oil in both quads. Erin is up at

the house," he answered. "Was that Dan in the truck with you?"

"Yeah. I picked him up in town. He's been out running and I found him in the bookstore. I twisted his arm a little to get him in the truck," she admitted, grinning. "He'd already done ten miles in this heat and it wasn't that hard to convince him that it was too hot to run another three miles."

"He probably wanted a ride in Big Blue" Eric said, pushing the tailgate up and into place with a loud bang.

Lydia grinned at him as she climbed back into the cab. "Not everybody is as impressed by this truck as you are. See you later," she called as she pulled the truck away from the building.

Chapter Ten

The black-and-white sheriff's patrol car cruised down the driveway and pulled up by the back door of the farmhouse. Lydia barely looked up from setting the table on the porch for dinner. She knew who it was and sighed. Butch Fraleigh had gone through school with her brother and although she had dated him only a few times while she was in college, he oozed possessiveness when he was around her and it drove her crazy.

She looked up with a smile and called out a "Hi" as he stepped up onto the porch. He greeted her with a big hug that lasted a touch too long and she poked him in the chest with the forks she held in her hand, making him step back.

"How's the crime-stopping business, Butch?" she asked as she turned back to the table.

"Keeping me busy, Lyddy," he answered, lowering himself into a chair and propping his feet up on another one. "Haven't seen you in a while. I know your parents are away and you're here alone, running things."

Lydia glanced at him as she put napkins at each place. "What makes you think I'm here alone? I'm sure your sources let you know that Erin and Eric are with me," she said as she leaned back against the edge of the table, regarding him with her eyebrows raised. "Did your source also tell you that we have a tenant living in the cottage?"

"Yeah, as a matter of fact." He frowned at her. "What do you know about him?"

"Enough," she said, a touch of impatience edging her voice. "He's a writer."

"Is that what he told you? Seems kind of funny for a writer to find this little town and know that your cottage was empty, doesn't it?" His voice was heavy with suspicion.

"What I think is that you've been playing Junior G-man too long and it's made you too suspicious," Lydia replied. "There's no reason to not believe him. He stays at the cottage all day and I assume he's writing. He told me he was working on the final rewrite of a book. He comes up here for dinner. End of story."

Butch narrowed his eyes. "He's met up with the same guy in town at least twice that I know of. Both of them are new in town, which looks a little odd to me." He paused. "Off the record, there's been some noise about increased drug traffic in the county. We don't expect the DEA to let the local Sheriff's Department in on anything," he said, a hint of resentment in his voice, "but we're not exactly blind to what's going on around here."

"Well, lose your concern about this guy. His parents are friends of Uncle Mark and I checked it with him before I let him take the cottage." She smiled at him. "Uncle Mark and Aunt Susan vouched for him. In fact, that's who told him about the cottage." She moved away from the table. "Thanks for your concern, though it's unnecessary."

Lydia heard a soft footstep outside the porch door and looked over to see Dan pulling the screened door open. She smiled at him and tried to ignore the dimple in his cheek as he smiled back. She made the introductions and watched with interest as Butch's cop facade fell into place. Dan stood, relaxed, while Butch seemed to exude tension. Interesting, she thought.

"Lydia says you're a writer." Butch's tone was challenging.

"Yes. I've been working on the rewrite all day and it's pretty boring." Dan's voice gave nothing away and didn't invite more questions.

Butch was in cop mode, though, and Lydia sighed. She thought she could smell the testosterone and set out to head Butch off. "Dan's latest book was published six months ago. Eric has a copy if you'd like to read it, Butch," she said, knowing well that he rarely read anything other than hunting and gun magazines. "By the way," she added, "will you stay for dinner? It's just waffles," neglecting to add the enticement of fresh strawberries, vanilla ice cream, and whipped cream that Erin was assembling in the kitchen.

Butch shook his head. "Thanks, but I've got to get going."

Dan went around the table and distributed the glasses and filled each one with iced tea from the pitcher. He set a napkin under the pitcher to catch the drips of condensation and looked over to Lydia.

"You need anything else done here?" he asked and, when she shook her head, walked into the kitchen. They could hear his voice, teasing Erin about her culinary abilities.

Butch's eyebrows drew together. "Pretty familiar, isn't he?"

"He's a nice guy, Butch," Lydia assured him.

"Maybe. Call me if you notice anything out of the ordinary."

"You bet, Butch," she muttered as she pulled back from the kiss he tried to land on her lips.

She watched him climb into the patrol car and heard the tires squeal as he gunned the engine, turning around and then speeding out the driveway.

She saw Dan pick up a huge bowl of sliced strawberries in one hand and another bowl heaped with whipped cream in the other. A few seconds later, he stepped out onto the porch and deposited them on the table. She could hear Erin calling to Eric and moved toward the kitchen to retrieve the bowl of ice cream she knew was resting in the freezer. Erin beat her to it, and as she pulled the bowl from the freezer compartment of the refrigerator and turned to hand it to Lydia, she asked, "What did Butch, the Super Cop, want?"

"Nothing much. It seems the local news service told him there was somebody living in the cottage and he came to check it out," Lydia answered.

"That's pretty nervy, don't you think? I mean, he has no business sticking his nose in your business, does he?" Erin continued, picking up the plate stacked high with waffles she had been keeping warm in the oven. "Does he think you have no brains and the little woman needs protecting or something?"

Dan raised his eyebrows at her as she sat down at the table. "If he does, he's a fool," he murmured in her ear.

Erin grinned at him. "He's one of those cops who thinks he's so in charge of everything. And he drives too fast and pushes the edge of the law just because he's a cop and thinks he can get away with it," she said.

"Careful, Erin. He has ambitions to take over the sheriff's job someday. He's just made detective and he's schmoozing the people with political connections that can help him." Lydia paused. "He might succeed too."

Eric dropped into a chair across from his sister.

"You're just still mad because he busted you for riding your bike without a helmet last summer."

"Not so," Erin denied vehemently. "He's too aggressive in everything." She turned to Lydia. "You agree with me, don't you?"

"As a matter of fact, I do. But, remember, he's also an old friend, so don't let it get back to him, okay?" She grinned.

Dan continued to help himself from the dishes being passed around, piling a mountain of strawberries on his waffle and topping it with ice cream and a dollop of whipped cream. He hid his interest in Lydia's answer by taking a huge bite of the waffle with its topping and chewing and then sighing. "Ambrosia," he said to Erin.

"Hey, wait a minute. I picked those berries. Give me some of the credit," Lydia teased, hoping to divert everyone's interest away from Butch. His cop persona annoyed her and the fact that she had once dated him annoyed her, but hey, she thought, *I was young and dumb then.* She glanced at Dan from the corner of her eye and couldn't detect any sign of interest in her dating history. Well, why should he care who she had dated? She didn't care about his previous girlfriends. Right, she sighed.

They were engaged in a "to the death" game of Scrabble when Dan's cell phone rang. Lydia advised him to take it in the kitchen or he'd never hear over the noise the twins were making in their argument about the validity of a word. He stepped into the kitchen, turned his back, and slid the phone from his shirt pocket. Lydia was watching him, ignoring the squabbling between brother and sister, and she saw his shoulders tense. He said a few more words, snapped the phone closed, and returned it to his pocket before coming back out on the porch.

"Sorry. I have to go," he said, interrupting the argument. "Something's come up. Thanks for dinner."

Lydia didn't ask any questions, merely nodded at him and then smiled when he looked right at her.

"See you guys tomorrow," he said over his shoulder as he stepped out the screen door and let it bang behind him. His footsteps rapidly faded away.

Erin broke off her argument with her brother to ask, "What's up with Dan? He was winning this game."

"Don't know," Lydia replied. His quick departure disturbed her a little. She was afraid there was trouble brewing. She had heard the seaplane landing and taking off again before they sat down to dinner and suspected the phone call was somehow related.

The headlights of a car driving away from the cottage caught her attention. It was too dark to see the car itself but she knew it was Dan's nondescript vehicle. The twins didn't seem to notice. They were setting up the board for a new game when she turned back to them.

An hour later, she was sitting in front of her computer, the monitor casting a bluish light on her face. It was the only light in the room, and she was not looking at the screen. Instead, she was looking out the window facing the cottage driveway, waiting.

When she saw headlights turn down the drive, she reached over and shut down the computer, stood, and walked into the kitchen. Erin was just putting the ingredients for a loaf of bread into the bread maker. She smiled at Lydia. "I'm going to put this on the timer so we'll have fresh bread in the morning. I made a batch of refrigerator jam out of the last of the strawberries and thought fresh bread and strawberry jam would be good for breakfast."

"Sounds good. I'm just going for a quick walk. I'll lock up when I get back, okay?"

"Sure," Erin said. "Say hi to Dan for me."

"Hey, you're supposed to be a self-absorbed teenager," Lydia said and laughed, "and not notice anything."

Erin snorted and turned back to the counter, reaching for the measuring spoons.

The lights were off in Dan's cottage but Lydia could see him sitting on the porch swing as she approached.

"I wondered if your curiosity would send you here," he remarked as she got to the bottom of the steps. "Come on up," he added when she hesitated. He pulled her down next to him when she tried to pass him to lean on the rail. His arm was warm around her shoulder.

"Just checking on my tenant," she protested, and she could feel him laugh.

"Right," he said.

"So, are you going to tell me what that was about, or not?" she asked.

He spoke slowly. "You've probably figured out that I have a partner on this little gig. You saw him in town and again today. Your cop boyfriend thinks I'm up to something. By the way," he added, "thanks for supporting my cover story."

Lydia shifted under his arm. "He's a former boyfriend, like in ancient history, Dan."

His hand was warm on her shoulder and he tugged her a little closer.

"The cop was pretty close, except that we're the good guys," he explained.

"Are you going to tell me about tonight?" she asked. "The other stuff I already guessed."

"The guy who was retrieving the drop-off from the plane and then stashing it for the pickup had a little 'accident.' Kevin tailed him tonight and our friend met up with somebody in the woods who obviously didn't like the way his face was arranged and rearranged it for him. Kevin created a little diversion and the guy left before he could beat Billy to death." He shrugged. "Kevin thinks Billy has been helping himself before he stashes the package. I can't believe anybody could be so stupid as to mess with a drug pickup and not expect to get killed for his efforts."

"If it's Billy Denzel you're talking about, you can believe it," Lydia remarked dryly. "Where's Billy now?" she asked.

"At the hospital, getting his nose set and his jaw wired. We dropped him off there and left." Dan laughed softly. "No sense letting the Sheriff's Department know we were anywhere around."

"Was he carrying any of the stuff when your friend got to him?"

"Nope. The goon was going through his pockets when Kevin got there. More than likely he removed anything Billy had on him. Billy didn't have time to hide it anywhere except in the hunting cabin where he left off the main package. We found that, but nothing else."

"Are you sure it was the buyer's bully who got to Billy?" Lydia looked at him, her eyes worried. "Could somebody else have figured out what was going on?"

"Maybe," Dan said. "Why would they stop at taking a small amount from Billy when they could have taken the whole delivery?"

"Maybe he's smart enough to know he'd definitely get killed if he stole the whole lot, and knows Billy's been getting away with lifting a small amount at a time, so it would be much safer. Of course," she continued, "if the whole delivery went missing, the buyer would go after Billy first. I don't know," she said, shaking her head.

"The guy, whoever it was, seems to have been on

foot. No sign of a vehicle." Dan said. "We'll look again in the morning."

"Are you saying it's another local who beat up on Billy?"

"Maybe," Dan admitted.

"How dangerous is this?" Lydia leaned toward him, bringing her shoulder against his. His fingers were making gentle circles around her shoulder and he turned his head to look directly at her.

"We're just here for information gathering. When the boss is ready to move, some more folks will show up." He didn't tell her about the armed passenger in the SUV or the possibility that he could be spotted up in his tree.

"I bet that scar on the back of your shoulder didn't come from falling out of a tree."

"Would you believe from falling off my skateboard?" He laughed, pulling her closer.

"No, and stop trying to distract me," she said, trying to push away from him.

"Am I distracting you?" he murmured as he touched his lips to the skin under her ear.

"Yes," she breathed as his lips feathered along her cheekbone and stopped at the corner of her mouth. "But if you don't tell me how you really got that scar, I'll just go on believing it was a bullet wound," she whispered.

He turned slightly, still holding her with his arm around her shoulders, his hand warm through her shirt. Her hand was caught against his chest as he kissed her gently. He was seducing her, she thought. She stopped breathing for a second, not encouraging him, but not rejecting him either. He pulled back and smiled at her. She stared into his eyes, eyes that made her feel warm and soft inside. It took her another minute to gather herself together. "I have to go now," she whispered.

"Yeah, you better," he agreed. "I'll walk you," he said.

"No. Flirt's with me," she said as she slowly pulled away and got to her feet. She walked down the steps and turned back to look at him. He was standing at the top of the steps. She thought he was smiling at her but it was too dark to be sure. There was a smile in his voice as he said good night. She called to Flirt and he saw the dog move from under a tree and join her as she walked down the driveway.

She *definitely* should have stayed at home and not let her nosiness get the better of her, she thought. It was much too easy to fall into daydreams here, with a sexy guy kissing her in the night, and her liking it very much. But why shouldn't she? He appeared to like her, and she liked him, so what was her problem? Was she worried about falling in love with someone who would be moving on in a short time? She didn't think so. In fact, she thought, she wasn't worried about anything, except now, maybe, his safety.

She looked down at Flirt, padding silently beside her.

"You don't have these problems, do you?" she asked out loud. The dog turned her head to look at her. "No comment, huh?" she answered herself, leaning down to rub her hand over the dog's head.

Chapter Eleven

The bed was comfortable and Dan wanted nothing more than to stay there a few more hours. His watch kept beeping in his ear, annoying enough to make him roll over and look at the clock on the little table. Yep, he thought. It was definitely one-thirty in the morning. His mind drifted to soft kisses and dark nights. He pushed himself up and swung his feet to the floor, tucking away the memory. Kevin would be waiting, grumbling about his sore butt and endless boredom.

After pulling on his clothes in the dark and grabbing his pack and retrieving the Glock from the drawer, he let himself out and silently started down the driveway. He paused, alert to a sound off to his right, and then relaxed and moved on when he saw a raccoon scurry off.

In fifteen minutes, he was circling around and

entering the woods north of their observation tree. He found Kevin crouched against the trunk of the tree and without a word, Kevin disappeared into the brush.

It was hard to stay focused during these long watches, but Dan settled himself as comfortably as he could against the tree, and did a quick survey of the area. The night-vision goggles made all the difference, with so little moonlight filtering through the dense canopy of the trees. An hour into his watch, he saw a pair of coyotes moving silently toward the north. They looked like the pair he had seen before, one a little bigger than the other, each moving steadily, keeping a hundred feet between their parallel paths.

The night went slowly after sighting the pair of coyotes. At five, he saw them heading back south, either unaware of, or unconcerned with, his presence in the tree. There was no sign of Billy, of course, but at five-thirty the black SUV again glided slowly toward the shack. The same figure, carrying a gun, got out of the vehicle, entered the building, and came back out in seconds, stuffing a package into his jacket pocket. As soon as the door was closed, the SUV backed around and moved out the dirt trail.

Billy had hidden the package in the shack before he was beaten up. Dan shook his head, thinking that Billy was lucky not to have been beaten to death this time. It was possible that his employers would dispose of him as a liability, or maybe Lydia was right in thinking that there was another player in this game.

A closer look at the locals wouldn't hurt. He'd probably start with Billy's coworker. He had a history of violence and local rumor had it that the two of them had gotten into a shoving match fairly recently, with some punches thrown over something stupid, like who was going to hook the manure spreader to the tractor.

Dan waited until the eastern sky was bright before packing his gear and lowering himself from the tree. He wanted to take a look around the area where Kevin had found Billy last night. It was light enough now to see easily and he moved quickly through the woods toward the airport. He spotted the rock formation just below the edge of the runway that Kevin had described. Below the overhang, he found a tiny piece of cloth that he thought matched the tattered shirt that Billy had been wearing, and right next to it was a clump of half-burned tobacco. He picked both up with a plastic bag from his vest pocket.

He grinned as he searched the ground again, noting the disturbed dirt and leaf duff, but finding nothing more out of place. That tobacco told him that the attacker was most likely Robert, the dairyman who stabbed cows with a pitchfork. Dan had seen the pipe clenched in his teeth while he was driving the tractor out in the hay field.

Fifteen minutes later he was in the cottage, calling in the information to his boss. Kevin could wait to hear this piece of news until he was slept out. He wouldn't appreciate a wake-up call at six in the morning for anything short of a nuclear holocaust.

Dan stripped off his clothes, hid the Glock under his T-shirts, and crashed on the bed.

Dan was sweating when he finally woke. His brain felt fuzzy and he had to stare hard at his watch to see the time. Noon already. He groaned, rolling off the bed. A cool shower should wake him up, he thought, and headed for the bathroom.

He was showered, shaved, and dressed in ten minutes and rummaged in the refrigerator for something to eat. Milk and a slab of cheese would have to do.

Kevin picked up on the first ring. Dan told him about the dottle of tobacco he had found and Kevin grunted in satisfaction before he said, "The state police have been brought in and are going to pick up Robert on possession charges. He's got the stuff in his house." He paused and Dan could imagine him shaking his head. "Sometimes the stupidity is mind-boggling," he commented. "The state police can hold him for a while on drug possession charges. Billy's in ICU. Probably going to have his jaw wired." He laughed softly. "Seems he was lifting some of the merchandise and his fourteen-year-old kid was selling it to somebody he knew. Robert got jealous."

Dan sat outside on the swing after Kevin hung up to eat some lunch, and saw Eric start down the lane on the quad, kicking up dust as he accelerated. It hadn't rained since the thunderstorm the other day and that hadn't amounted to much in terms of actual rainfall. From his vantage point, he could see over practically the whole farm. The pond sparkled in the sun and the apple orchard beyond was a deep green. Not a leaf stirred in the still air. He wouldn't be surprised if another thunderstorm rolled this way later in the day.

He went back inside and rinsed his glass at the sink, picked up his keys, and went out to the car. He had seen Erin and Lydia going into a building that, in addition to a lot of windows, had a garage door centered in its side. He had no idea what was in that building and was curious, but he wasn't ready to be quizzed about last night's activities. Avoiding Lydia right now was the thing to do, he thought regretfully. He figured Lydia would know he had been on surveillance this morning. She knew that the seaplane had landed and taken off from the airport and she knew Billy had been beaten. He was pretty sure she wouldn't be able to contain her curiosity for long.

He put the car in gear and drove out of the farm and turned toward the village, intending to make a quick run to the grocery store. He passed Irv's farm and noticed the cows, all standing in the shade of a couple of trees near the creek or standing in the water. It looked placid and timeless, the cows chewing cud and swishing their tails, unconcerned with anything but their own small world. It occurred to him that he had never met the owner, but figured he would soon, since two of his employees were very much involved in this case.

The cold air inside the store was welcome, and while he put things in his cart, he turned over ways to get close to Irv without blowing his cover.

He still hadn't decided on a plan when he pulled into the farm driveway. Lydia and Erin were standing outside the big garage door, in the shade cast by the building. Both of them looked hot and Dan stopped the car next to them. Erin leaned in the open window. "We're going to take the boat out later. Want to come?" she asked.

"Count on it," he replied, grinning at her. Lydia bent down until she could look in.

"We're going up to Irv's at four o'clock. He needs help with the milking. His wife just called to tell me that Billy got hurt last night and is in the hospital, and Robert, his dairyman, was arrested for something or other. She didn't know the details, she said."

Dan tried to look interested and innocent at the same time. She had just presented him with the solution and he jumped on it.

"Mind if I come along?" he asked. "I'd like to see how it's done."

Lydia's grin was quizzical as she nodded and stepped back.

"We'll pick you up at four, then," she agreed, a knowing grin on her face.

Dan left his car in the shade next to the cottage and carried the bag of groceries inside, then booted up his laptop. Time to get something done on this rewrite, he thought. There were a couple of hours before he could expect to be picked up and he really needed to get moving on this.

He had changed his shorts for a pair of jeans and was diligently editing the manuscript on his laptop when he heard the sound of the SUV's engine coming up the lane. He saved the file and shut down the computer before grabbing a cap and jamming it on his head. He was out on the porch when Lydia came to a stop and he ran down the stairs and climbed in the backseat next to Eric.

Lydia looked at him in the rearview mirror. "We've got to get you a Ford Tractor or a John Deere hat," she said, grinning at him. He turned to look at Eric and saw a billed cap advertising a feed company, and Erin, in the front seat, flipped hers around to show him the logo of the local farm supply store.

"If you're going to hang with us, you have to dress the part or Irv will start yanking your chain about being a city slicker. He can be brutal." Lydia laughed. "He knows you're coming, by the way. I told him you were visiting and had never seen a cow milked. He usually only does the morning milking, but with Robert out of the picture for now, I expect he'll be there for the evening chores." She glanced over her shoulder at him. "I used to milk for him when I was in high school and summers during college so I know his system."

She pulled up near a big, red-painted barn, leaving

the SUV in the shade of a huge maple tree. The cows were waiting patiently in an enclosure, their tails swishing rhythmically. Erin walked over and climbed the bottom board of the fence so she could scratch the topknot of a doe-eyed brown cow watching them. "That's a Jersey," Lydia said, nodding toward the animal. "Irv keeps a few to help the butterfat content."

She saw the slightly confused look on Dan's face and explained. "The Holsteins, the black-and-white cows in this herd, produce huge volumes of milk but the butterfat content is not nearly as high as in the milk produced by a Jersey. The Jerseys, like that little brown one, produce a milk that's much higher in butterfat content but the volume of production is much less per cow. And since the payment scheme includes a premium for butterfat . . ." She shrugged.

"Got it, I think," Dan said. "Tell me what to do here. I'm willing, but ignorant."

"Let me give you a quick tour before the cows come in," she said, touching his arm and stepping up onto a stone porch and pulling open the screen door. The room they entered was cool and contained two huge stainless-steel vats with pipes leading to them.

"This is the milk room. The cows are milked by machine and the milk flows to these vats, which cool it down and hold it for pickup by the trucks you've probably seen on the highway. They pick up here every other day. This whole operation is inspected periodically and the milk is tested. The trucks are compartmentalized so the milk from one farm is kept separate from the milk from another until it's been tested at the facility for antibiotic contamination, cell count, and for protein and butterfat content, before it's processed."

She led the way into the main part of the barn and pointed out the stanchions and head catches. "Irv has never gone to a free-stall barn. He still milks in this old stanchion barn. At least he went to a pipeline collection system and got rid of the old vacuum pails. They were easy to contaminate because you had to pour the milk from each cow into a bigger container for it to be sucked into the tanks in the milk room. It's still done that way at a couple of small farms around here but it's a lot of extra work."

Dan could see Eric pushing a huge cart in front of the row of stanchions, dumping feed on the concrete in front of each head gate. Erin was moving along the row, testing the water cups, and grinned over at Lydia. "We're ready to let them in whenever you give the word."

Lydia gave Erin a thumbs-up and walked to the end of the row. A minute later, the cows started moving in, some of them pushing to get into position. Erin and Eric moved along, closing the head catch as a cow stuck her head through and started eating. "We've done this before for Irv, so the kids know their job," she said to Dan above the noise made by a hundred cows eating.

He leaned down, his ear close to her mouth, to catch her words as the sound of the motors of the milking machine kicked on.

Lydia slid her hand around Dan's arm. "Just stick with me. The cows don't kick backward, so you'll be safe behind them. Basically, the udder is cleaned, the vacuum cups are attached to the teats and the machine does the milking. I talk to them and touch them so they know where I am and what I'm doing."

To Dan, the cow seemed perfectly unconcerned, maybe even grateful for the relief provided by the removal of the pressure inside the udder from the volume of milk.

Lydia repeated the process with the next cow and then moved across the aisle to hook up the first two in that row. She had four cows milking simultaneously. When they were milked out, she repeated the process with the next four and moved down the rows in a gentle rhythm. Dan noticed she worked efficiently but quietly, always talking to the cows, never letting one get uncomfortable from the sucking of the vacuum, keeping the cows calm.

Dan looked away from Lydia and noticed a short, rotund man making his way toward them, stopping behind one cow and reaching under her. He grunted when he stood upright, took a syringe from behind his ear, and slapped the cow on the rump before plunging the needle in. The cow didn't lift her head from the feed in front of her and the syringe again went behind his ear, riding there like a pencil.

Lydia paused long enough to greet him. "Hey, Irv, the cows look good."

"Yeah. There are a couple on antibiotics, though. They're marked." He looked at Dan. "Who's this young feller?" he asked, looking Dan over. "New boyfriend, heh?"

"Behave yourself, Irving, or I'll tell Kay," Lydia ordered. "This is Dan. He's visiting on the farm. Knows Uncle Mark down in Annapolis."

Dan noticed that Lydia's speech had slipped into the cadence and language pattern of the old farmer. Irv nodded at him. "Nice girl, here. You couldn't find better. About the best milker I ever seen," he confided. "Almost glad that damn Robert got hisself arrested!"

Dan raised his eyebrows. "Your help got arrested?"

"Yup. State police were around, askin' questions. Found some drugs over at his house, dumb bugger." He shook his head. "If anybody had asked me, I'd a thought it was Billy doin' somethin' stupid. He's been flashing a little too much money around and my wife asked me about it." He shook his head. "Don't need no drug trouble here. I got grandkids come to visit all the time."

Lydia looked around. "Billy's in the hospital, I hear. What happened?"

"Fool got beat up. Says he doesn't know who did it, but that's a lie," he snorted. "My money's on Robert."

Lydia smiled as she bent to the next cow in the row. "Well, since I've never known you to lose money, I'll bet you're right. Did Robert say anything?"

"Nope, but he was wearin' a black eye early this mornin'." Irv grinned at Dan, showing yellowed teeth and an evil expression. "Guess they nailed him, huh? And he'll wait a long time before I'll bail him out, even if I have to sell every blasted cow. I'm not puttin' up with that crap around here," he growled. He moved farther along the row of cows, stopping to check an udder on a cow with a big red mark on her rump.

Lydia looked over at Dan. "He's really pretty easygoing with the men, but this time, I think they've pushed too far. He'll stick to his guns, at least for a few days, while we do the milking for him." She glanced in Irv's direction. "You need anything else from him?" she asked, grinning at him.

"Man, I can't get away with anything with you, can I?" he grinned.

"Pretty much, but don't let the dumb old farmer routine fool you. He's got a mind like a steel trap and he doesn't miss anything, so if he thinks Robert beat up Billy, you can bet the farm on it." She looked around and Dan realized they had reached the end of the row of cows. "We're done with these ladies," she said, nodding toward the rows of cows. "Just a couple more," she added. "The ones on antibiotics get milked separately and the milk fed to some veal calves he's raising," she said as she walked back down the line of cows.

Dan trailed behind, watching a skinny old man plying a shovel at the back end of the cows, scraping manure into the gutter running behind the cows. He saw Lydia greet the man, who laughed and then bent over, coughing. As he approached them, Lydia introduced him to Fred, while patting Fred on the back to ease the coughing spell. "Fred has emphysema and still smokes, right Fred?" she asked.

"No use stoppin' now," he groused, leaning on his shovel while he caught his breath. He started coughing again and Lydia patted him on the back before walking away.

She waited for Dan at the end of the aisle. "No way he's part of whatever you're here for. He can hardly breathe enough to walk," she said to Dan.

He looked at her with his left eyebrow raised. "You're not involved, remember?"

"Oh, right," she said, smiling at him. "Come on. It looks like Eric already milked the antibiotic cows and he and Erin are feeding the calves." She stretched her arms above her head and groaned and Dan admired her curves while she did it. She saw him looking and he was sure she blushed. She turned away, saying, "I'm ready for the river. I'll see if the twins are done. Fred and Irv will let the cows out."

Chapter Twelve

The twins were leaning against the SUV when Lydia came out into the bright sunlight. It was much hotter out here than it had been in the barn with the big fans running, she realized. "I'm more than ready for a swim," she said as Dan walked next to her. "I like milking but I'm sure glad I don't do it for a living." She sighed.

"That setup makes life harder than it has to be, doesn't it?" Dan asked.

"Yeah, but Irv's so tight he's still got the first dollar he ever made, selling chickens when he was eight years old, and he won't spend any money. He makes the word 'tightwad' seem like a compliment!"

Dan got in the front of the SUV, pulling his hat off and wiping his face with the bottom of his shirt.

Lydia looked over at him, smiling. "Time for the river, I'd say." Her face was shiny with sweat and her T-shirt was plastered to her back. She leaned forward in her seat as she started the engine, reaching behind her to pull the material away from her back. "I'm whacked," she admitted. "All that bending was okay when I was eighteen, but now I'd prefer it if Irving would spring for a parlor setup." She glanced over at Dan. "You get to stand below the cows then. No bending."

Dan reached toward the air vents and adjusted them so they all blew directly on Lydia. The air conditioner was starting to spew out cold air and Dan reached across and pinched the material at the front of her T-shirt and lifted it away from her chest. She looked startled for a minute and then grinned. "That helps. Thanks."

"Pick you up in ten, okay?" Lydia said five minutes later as she stopped at the foot of the cottage driveway to let him out. He nodded and watched her drive away.

Lydia and the twins were back in ten minutes, trailering the boat. Eric tossed Dan's duffel bag in the back and grinned at him as he climbed in the front seat. "We've got the skis with us. You up for a lesson?"

"You bet." Dan looked over at Lydia, smiling. "You the teacher?"

"I'm the driver. I get to watch you crash and burn." She grinned.

He laughed and reached over to lay his hand on her bare thigh. "I'm a good downhill skier. Will that help me?"

"Most likely," she said, glancing down at his hand. "However, just remember that the driver can make or break you," she warned. She felt his hand slide toward her knee and risked a quick look at him. He was smiling at her, his eyes warm, and she wiggled in her seat. Her skin felt cold for a second, after he removed his hand.

It was already six o'clock but it was still hot, even down near the water. The sky was cloudless and the air was still. Ten minutes later, they were out on the river and Lydia was slowing the boat to idle before shutting it down completely. She pulled her shirt over her head, dropped her shorts, and was over the side of the boat and into the water in seconds. Her head popped up a minute later, and she laughed. "Come on in. Man, I feel better already," she said, just before she sank below the surface.

Dan and the twins were in the water before she surfaced twenty yards away. Dan met her as she swam back toward the boat, her arms flashing in the sunlight. Dan treaded water, admiring the smooth curve of her back as she dove under the water again. Erin and Eric were racing each other around the boat, each trying to maneuver the other out from the boat to gain an advantage. They splashed up to him just as Lydia surfaced again. This time she turned on to her back and floated toward them.

Eric swam back to the boat, calling, "I'll get the skis ready," before pulling himself over the side.

Lydia floated up next to Dan, moving her hands and feet to maneuver herself next to him. She smiled at him. "Want to try the skis? I'm pretty well cooled off now."

"Sure," he said, turning toward the boat. She got to the boat before him and he got to watch the flexing muscles of her back and legs as she climbed over the side. Now he was hot again, he thought, treading water for a minute before pulling himself over the side. Lydia had dragged an oversized T-shirt over her suit and he sighed with regret. The view had been *very* fine indeed.

Eric tossed the towrope into the water and rolled over the side, holding the skis. "I'll show you how it's done, then you can try, okay?" he called. Dan nodded and sat at the stern, listening to the sound of the engine as Lydia started it and slowly moved forward. Eric positioned the skis on his feet, holding the towrope. His orange life vest was easily visible in the water and he raised his arm when he was ready. The boat moved forward, picking up speed. Eric came into an upright position, the skis leaving trails of their own inside the wake of the boat. The boat started into a wide curve and Eric rode over its wake, making it look easy.

Eric collapsed back into the water as Lydia slowed the boat and Erin tossed Dan a life jacket saying, "The hard part is getting up out of the water without crashing." She grinned at him. "Your turn."

He got up on the first try, a little wobbly but up. Trying to remember to keep his center of gravity behind the skis, he hung onto the towrope, enjoying the speed. The pull on his arms was more than he had anticipated and after a few minutes, his thighs started to ache from the effort of staying upright and in control. The boat swung into a wide arc and he went over the wake like he was riding a mogul at Aspen. This was definitely a fun sport, he thought. He was feeling very smug when Lydia suddenly slowed the boat. The towrope slackened and his body weight went forward and he collapsed into the water. Lydia brought the boat around slowly and he grinned up at Erin, who was leaning over the side.

"Lydia says that's enough for the first time or your legs are gonna kill you," she yelled over the noise of the engine. She rolled over the side and popped up next to him, grinning.

"My turn," she said, reaching for the skis. "You're pretty good, you know."

Dan grinned back at her before swimming to the boat and hauling himself over the side. When he stood up, his legs felt a little rubbery and he bent over to massage his thighs before he unfastened the vest and pulled it off.

He looked up to see Lydia watching from her place at the wheel and gave her a grin before grabbing a towel from the bench and drying himself off. With a shirt pulled over his chest, he went to stand next to her at the wheel as she revved the engine, putting the boat in motion again. Eric was at the back, watching Erin, alert for any sign of trouble. "He's a good spotter, so I don't have to watch," she told him, looking ahead, watching a speedboat paralleling their course and sending a wake toward them. "That's going to cause some turbulence for Erin," she said, just as Eric yelled. She immediately cut their speed and circled back to Erin, floating a hundred yards behind, her flotation vest pinpointing her position in the water.

Erin gave them a wave as they came close and Eric tossed the towrope back into the water next to her. She was up again as soon as Lydia had the boat moving, gliding back and forth across the boat's wake with ease. Lydia took the boat into a wide circle and finally slowed, allowing Erin to sink back into the water before turning back to pick her up.

The sun was much lower on the horizon now and Erin was shivering a little as she climbed over the side. "That was fun, Lydia," she called, removing the bright-orange vest and rubbing herself dry with a towel. Dan pulled a sweatshirt out of his bag and handed it to her as she came forward. She pulled it over her head and then hugged Lydia from behind.

"You guys had enough?" Lydia asked, looking over her shoulder at Erin standing behind her.

When she nodded, Lydia throttled up, bringing the boat in a wide arc. They had gotten almost to the bridge spanning the river and she headed upstream to bring them back to the dock. The air was definitely cooler now. The sun was still a ways above the horizon and the mountains stood out sharply in the clear air. It was one of the prettiest spots Dan could remember seeing, all sparkling water, blue sky, and tree-covered mountains. Definitely a nice place to be on a hot summer day, Dan thought.

Lydia looked over at him, smiling. Yeah, definitely a nice place to be, he thought, as he smiled back. It took him a few seconds to take in what she was saying.

"It's pizza night. You have any preferences?"

He had a preference for a smart, focused, pretty woman wearing a Speedo but that wasn't what she was asking. She glanced away and he was aware that his own eyes were too intense as he looked at her. *Think about pizza here, dummy!* He shook his head and draped his arm over her shoulders. She didn't pull away, but leaned slightly against him. He looked over his shoulder at Erin and winked. She gave him a quick smile before walking to the back of the boat and sitting beside Eric.

Lydia was concentrating on guiding the boat toward the dock but was very aware of Dan's arm sliding down her back and his hand resting at her waist. "You warm enough?" he said in her ear.

"Oh, yeah," she said, turning her head slightly toward him. "Quit distracting me for a minute while I get us up to the dock."

"Okay, but only for a minute," he whispered into her ear as the engine sound died. He took his arm away and stepped behind her as she let the boat drift to the dock and he turned to see Eric jump off and secure them to the piling.

"Time for more distraction," he said as he bent to kiss the nape of her neck. Her ponytail tickled his nose and he smiled as she turned around, hoping she wasn't going to slap him. She didn't; she kissed him lightly on the lips instead.

"Come on," she murmured, and he followed her off the boat, thinking more of kissing her than walking, and when he stumbled off the edge of the dock, he looked up to see her grinning at him. She grabbed his arm and pulled him toward the SUV, parked on the other side of the parking area. "We'll be right back," Lydia called to Erin, noting the big smile splitting her face. "I think Erin is aiding and abetting you. Not that I'm complaining," she added, laughing. When they reached the big black monster, he pulled her around to the far side, out of sight, and backed her up against the door. When she just stood there, smiling, he slid one hand behind her head and touched the side of her face with the palm of his other hand before he brought his mouth close to hers. "Ready for some distraction now?" he whispered against her lips.

"More than ready." She sighed as she closed her eyes. Her lips were soft and sweet and he slid his hand down her back, pulling her closer. He was losing himself in the pleasure of kissing her when she pulled back slightly, placing a hand on his chest.

"We have to get the boat out of the water," she reminded him. Her eyes were half-closed and Lydia really didn't want to move. She'd rather stay here, kissing him all night. He grinned at her, and she wondered if he had just read her mind. He bent forward and brushed his lips over hers before stepping back.

"Time for the boat, the twins, and a pizza," he said. "Did I tell you I'm off duty for the next three days?" Dan asked as she moved toward the driver's side. He held the door for her and grinned suggestively at her as he closed it. He was sure that was a blush rising from the neck of her shirt and he grinned again before circling around to climb in the other side.

She turned to look at him before starting the engine and her smile was mischievous. "Good. You can help with Irving's morning milkings. Four A.M. all right with you?"

"That wasn't quite what I was thinking about," he admitted.

"How about harvesting garlic?" Lydia offered.

"Not that either," he admitted, laughing at her teasing tone.

"Well, how *did* you want to fill your days if not with work?" she asked, starting the engine and backing toward the loading ramp.

"With you." He looked at her, waiting.

He thought she wasn't going to say anything, but then she said, "Okay," and he leaned back, taking a deep breath. "Good."

Lydia heard him but concentrated on backing the trailer down the ramp. She reached for her cell phone, punched in a number, and ordered two pizzas with everything. Eric winched the boat into place and he and Erin secured it and tossed the skis and the rest of their gear into the back and climbed inside.

"You order yet, Lydia?" Eric asked. "I'm starved."

"Done," Lydia replied. "It'll be ready when we get there."

Dan groaned, rubbing his stomach. "I think I overate," he said to no one in particular, leaning back in his chair.

"Does that mean you concede that New York pizza is superior to any other?" Lydia asked. Her eyes were closed as she lay back in a wicker chair and Dan was admiring her legs, long and tan, as she lifted her feet onto the ottoman. She had changed into shorts and a T-shirt and looked half-asleep.

"Yeah. I concede. That was great," he said, sliding down in his chair.

It was quiet on the porch. The frogs at the pond were making their usual evening racket and he could hear the sound of the background bass booming from Eric's room upstairs. Erin had disappeared from the kitchen, leaving only the light over the sink burning. He heard the sound of a sheep coughing, and heard the border collie woof at something passing by.

It would be easy to fall sleep right where he sat but

it would be better if he got himself up, went to the cottage, and let Lydia go to bed. He remembered the four A.M. milking that she was to do in the morning and hauled himself to his feet. Lydia didn't stir and he thought she had fallen asleep, but when he bent over and lightly kissed her forehead, she opened her eyes.

"Pick me up in the morning. I'll help with the milking at Irv's," he said.

Lydia reached up and pulled on his arm, making him bend down to keep his balance. Her lips were warm on his for a second before she let go of his arm and he straightened up.

"Night, Dan. See you in the morning . . . early." She sighed. He watched her for a few seconds, her eyes closed again and her body relaxed. She was already sleeping when he let himself out the screened door. Flirt lifted her head long enough to acknowledge him and then returned her muzzle to its place on her front paws. A cat, its eyes shining in the light from the kitchen, crossed the lane as he walked away from the house. The frogs stopped their croaking for a few seconds and then resumed their chorus.

Chapter Thirteen

A light breeze had come up, making the branches
of the trees along the lane move almost languorously.
The temperature had dropped enough to make it
pleasant walking. It would be much more comfortable
sleeping tonight. That thought brought him back to the
image of Lydia sleeping in her chair. She worked physically hard and played just as hard and he realized how
tired she must have been to fall asleep in the chair
while he watched.

It would be very easy to move from like to love with
this woman and he wondered if he had already done
so. His other girlfriends had never had him counting
minutes until he could talk to them again.

He stopped for a second as he reached the bottom
of his porch steps, noticing the brightness of the stars

overhead. Clear again tomorrow, most likely. It would be an early morning but nothing unusual for him, considering his job. Maybe he could stay around for a while after this case was over. He was ready to use the excuse of finishing work on his book to make it seem reasonable to continue living in the cottage for a while. The urge to stay near Lydia unsettled him a little but went with the need to talk to her and just be with her. God, he was in deeper than he'd realized!

It was still dark when his watch alarm woke him. The cottage was cool and he rolled out of bed, dressed, and brushed his teeth without turning on any lights. His beard felt scratchy as he rubbed his face, knowing that he didn't have time to shave. He could see headlights turning onto the cottage driveway and he grabbed his hat off the desk and jammed it on his head.

Lydia grinned as he pulled open the passenger side door and climbed in beside her. Boy, he looked good: slightly rumpled, slightly sleepy, and more than slightly sexy. She tried to get her mind back on business but couldn't resist kissing him back when he leaned toward her and kissed her cheek, murmuring a good morning. And there went her good intentions. She had talked herself into believing that they were friends and only friends, but seeing him and kissing him good morning squashed that line of thinking and made her think beyond "friend." She leaned back in her seat, smiling at him in the darkness, able to see the smile on his face in the dim light from the dash.

"Where are our chaperones?"

"I left them sleeping. We're starting the garlic harvest this morning, so they'll be up when we get back." She headed down the driveway, glancing at him as he chuckled.

"No wonder you fall asleep over dinner," he said.

"I do not." She paused. "I wait until after dinner. Besides, I like what I'm doing. I assure you I don't live like this in my academic world."

"Does that statement mean you don't like the academic life?" he asked, turning to look at her.

"Truthfully, I loved it for a while. But I'm tired of it. Academics, I've found, are not in the real world, the world I grew up in, and I miss that. I found I missed getting up before dawn when the work called for it, sweating and getting dirty, helping the neighbors when they need it." She sighed. "So, when I finish this dissertation, I'm done. That's it," she said emphatically.

He was silent for a moment, sitting next to her. Then said, "But you'll keep working and documenting your work." He said this with conviction, and she had to smile.

"Oh, yeah. Sticking my oar in and stirring up the waters is one thing I do well. There's a whole world out there to publish in and that's what I intend to do." She paused as she pulled in front of the big dairy barn. "Pretty profound for this time of the morning, huh?"

"You're pretty amazing, I'd say," he answered, pushing open his door and getting out into the darkness.

The barn lights were on and casting a glow outside the open door. The sweet smell of silage greeted them as they stepped inside. Fred was pushing a feed cart along the aisle, pausing and struggling to deposit a forkful in front of each cow. Dan moved toward him when Lydia nodded at him. He greeted Fred cheerfully, relieving him of the fork. He had watched this drill just yesterday, and Dan proceeded to move forward and dump a huge quantity of feed under the nose of each cow. A tongue would snake out, wrapping around the pile, pulling the chopped feed into a slobbery mouth and then the jaws would start a sideways grinding motion.

Dan was fascinated by the eating ritual of a stanchioned dairy cow. The tongue action reminded him of a kid swiping his tongue at an ice cream cone. Apparently, the cows thought the stuff he put in front of them was just as tasty. He looked over his shoulder to see Lydia watching and he gave her a wave as he patted the topknot of the pretty little Jersey cow next in line.

He left the cart and fork at the end of the aisle and walked back to Fred. "What's next, Fred?"

"Just the calves. We gotta wait 'til the milkin's done for that." Fred coughed into a dirty bandanna he dragged from his back pocket. "Miss Lydia will tell me when she's ready for me." He walked out the main door and stood in the darkness, lighting a cigarette.

Dan looked around and spotted Lydia bending to attach the cups of the milking machine to a cow with the biggest udder he had ever seen. Must be painful, he thought, just as the cow lifted her foot in a quick kicking motion, Lydia blocked the motion with her other arm and slipped the teat cups into place. Dan had started toward her as the cow kicked but slowed when he saw the quick defensive move Lydia had used. Lydia never broke the rhythm of her motions and just kept talking to the cow as if nothing happened, although Dan had seen Lydia's arm fly upward with the force of the kick.

Dan reached for the cleaning cloth from the dispenser and was already washing the udder and teats of the next cow when Lydia straightened up and turned around. She grinned at him. "That cow always kicks. It's probably in her genes. Her mother was a kicker too."

Dan moved down the lines of cows, preparing the udders for the machine, staying one cow ahead of Lydia and the machine. Occasionally, a cow would shift her weight at the touch of the cold solution on the udder and Dan would tense, holding his arm ready to block any attempt at kicking forward, but none of the remaining animals offered him violence, for which he was grateful. He wasn't looking forward to having his brains bashed by a recalcitrant cow. He could hear Lydia's soothing voice as she greeted each animal and he found himself talking to them in the same way.

By the time they reached the last cow, he had mastered the art of not startling a cow, soothing her as he bent to wash her udder, and sympathizing with the discomfort each one was feeling at the pressure of an udder full of milk.

"You're hired," Lydia said as she stood next to him, waiting for the last two cows to empty their burden into the pulsating hoses.

He smiled. "I can appreciate the romance of this scene, but I can't say I'd want to do this for a living." He heard Lydia laugh, but before he could say anything else, she moved to bend toward the last cow and gently break the suction, dip the teats, and release the hose from the vacuum line.

She walked halfway down the line of cows and picked up the stainless-steel milking container, with its cover and attached hoses and dials, and then positioned it next to a cow with a big red *X* on her hip. "This one has had antibiotics so she's milked separately. There's one other to do after this one and then Fred will feed this milk to the calves."

When she straightened up from attaching the machine, she backed into Dan, who had been waiting for this opportunity. His arms closed around her waist and he kissed her ear. "This makes milking cows at four in the morning worth it," he said into her ear.

She leaned against him, enjoying the feel of his broad chest against her back. "Mm-hmm," she agreed as she felt his lips on the side of her neck.

"Hey, hey, no necking in my barn!"

Lydia straightened up, ending the contact, and looked around to see Irv walking toward them. His

overalls were stained with fresh blood and other stuff
that Dan preferred not to identify.

Lydia laughed at him. "Irving, you've been rolling
in the muck again! Kay is going to kill you when she
sees that mess. I suppose you'll expect her to clean it."

"Wonderful woman, my wife." He shook his head
at them. "A little calving problem but it's okay now.
You 'bout done here?"

"Just one more," Lydia said as she reached to remove
the machine from the udder and then carried the whole
unit to the other marked cow. Dan was ahead of her,
providing the cleaning necessary before she attached
the unit. As soon as the cow milked out, Irving shut
off the vacuum motor and bellowed for Fred to come
get the milk and feed the calves. The cows stopped
chewing for a second as the unexpected noise of Irving's shout filled the barn and then they returned to their
placid contemplation of the pile of feed in front of them.

The grin Irv sent Dan was purely lascivious and
Lydia smacked him on the arm. "You okay here? Tell
Kay hi for me, Irving. We'll be back this afternoon."

"Appreciate it, Lydia," he said, turning and immediately hollering for Fred again, grumbling under his
breath.

"One of the local characters, huh?" Dan remarked
as they walked to the SUV in the early light of dawn.
The sky was cloudless, the air still cool.

"You could say that." Lydia laughed. "His father
was a wheeler-dealer in the cattle business and Irving

learned the trade at his father's knee. Still tells some of the tales about his father's skill in making a buck off somebody's breakdown cow or outsmarting some other dealer."

"That's a pretty motley collection of workers he has," he commented as they settled in the seats. Later in the day, the vinyl seat covers would be hot enough to fry an egg but right now it felt cool against his back. He watched as Lydia searched for the end of the seat belt with her left hand and then drew it across herself and snapped it in place.

"I'm not sure if Irv keeps them employed out of the goodness of his heart, because they don't know anything else and none of them are exactly an asset in the industrial workforce," she said, shrugging, "or whether he keeps them because he can pay them practically nothing and get away with it. Of course, they supplement their income whenever Irv's not looking."

"Perfect conditions to make a man try something illegal if it meant getting some easy money." He frowned, thinking that being poor wasn't the only condition that would make a man look for an easy buck. Sometimes, greed was just greed.

Lydia was silent until they pulled up by the farmhouse. "Come in for breakfast. It's not even six yet and the twins won't be up for a while, but I do know how to scramble an egg."

"I know how to make coffee, so let me do that," Dan offered as they stepped into the kitchen. "I'd say

I was anxious to observe your cooking skills but the truth is I'm hungry and you're my best chance of getting a decent breakfast."

"I bet your mother waits on you at home," she grumbled, getting the egg carton out of the refrigerator.

"I was hardly ever home, so she didn't get the chance." He grinned at her. "I have an apartment on the top floor of the family house. We fixed it up that way when I started this job after college and it works because I've had to travel so much 'til now."

The frying pan was heating on the stove while Lydia stirred eggs in a bowl, and she looked over at him where he leaned against the counter. "You sound like you're done with traveling."

"Yeah. After this case, I'm quitting to write full time."

Lydia looked over her shoulder at him, her eyebrows raised.

"Time to settle down, I think," he said, holding her eyes until she turned away, dumping the eggs in the pan.

Lydia didn't say a thing, but her brain was in fifth gear, racing around the possibilities that his words presented. Settling down in her world meant a guy was intent on finding a wife, staying around home, and creating a family. She glanced over her shoulder to find him smiling at her. Now it was his turn to raise his eyebrows.

She could feel the heat rising in her face and concentrated on stirring the eggs in the pan, which were starting to burn around the edges! She yanked the pan away from the flame, muttering, "This is why I can't cook. I'm too easily distracted."

Dan laughed, taking the spatula from her and dishing the eggs onto a pair of plates he had retrieved from the cabinet. Lydia grabbed the toast out of the toaster oven just before *that* burned and managed to get it on a plate without dropping it. In the minute it took to get the butter and jam from the refrigerator and carry them to the kitchen table, she was able to control her face, if not her heart rate, and sit down looking composed. She thanked Dan when he poured coffee into the mug in front of her and decided to ignore the last few minutes.

Dan sat across from her and began eating. He figured she needed room, but he wasn't worried. He'd seen the blush and was sure she had gotten his not-very-subtle message. Time to back off a little and let the thought work its way through her brain. He had never felt this way about any woman—wanting to be with her, see her, take care of her, have a family with her. It was unsettling in some ways but felt good in others.

Chapter Fourteen

Lydia knew she would need a nap by afternoon and she slumped in her chair, clutching her second mug of coffee. The caffeine jolt wasn't enough. She could see Dan watching as she brought the mug to her mouth. He looked slightly disreputable, his beard dark, his hair mussed from his baseball cap, and his shirt frayed at the neck. Yum.

"We'll start on the garlic this morning," she said, pushing herself up from the chair. "Come by for lunch if you want. We'll stop by around noon when it gets too hot," she added. "Stay as long as you want," she said as she backed toward the dining room door.

He grinned at her, tipping his chair back on two legs. "I'm helping with the garlic."

"You are?"

"I told you I was free for the next few days. So I'm ready to help." He let his chair fall forward. "Don't you want me?"

Oh boy. It was too early in the morning to deal with that question. Instead, she smiled at him and suggested he catch a nap while she worked at the computer until the twins were up. "Use the couch in the living room, if you want. It's long enough," she said, eyeing his legs, stretched out in front of him. She swallowed hard and turned away. No way was she waiting to see if he took her up on that invitation. She retreated toward the office and booted up the computer, trying to ignore the look that went with his question.

She was working diligently on the data input when Erin banged on the doorjamb as she passed on her way to the kitchen. She had successfully ignored Dan's question but it surfaced now, pinching at her and making her feel restless.

Eric was pulling bottles of water out of the refrigerator and dropping them into the cooler when she reached the kitchen. Erin was putting dishes in the dishwasher and looked up at her. "You've got that glassy-eyed look that you get whenever you've been on the computer for a while."

"I know, I know. Where's Dan? He said he'd help with the garlic."

A big, warm hand rubbed up and down her back and she felt her ponytail being tweaked. So . . . now she knew where Dan was.

Erin grinned at her before slamming the dishwasher door closed. "We're ready when you are, Lydia. We just have to move the wagon into position."

The flatbed wagon had been rigged with poles at each corner and a white vinyl tarp was stretched over the poles. While Eric pulled it next to the garlic beds, Lydia pulled a bulb out of the ground. The top still had four green leaves; the others were brown and dry. With a couple of flicks of her hand, she brushed the dirt away from the root mass and bulb and held it up.

The bulb was at least two and a half inches in diameter and showed a few faint purple streaks in its creamy color. Lydia looked at Dan and grinned. "You won't find these at the grocery store. This is German hardneck, or stiffneck."

"That doesn't look anything like the stuff I've seen at home," Dan said, taking the bulb from her.

"The softneck varieties are what you find at the store. The softnecks last longer in storage and are easier to grow. The cognoscenti, me included, think the hardnecks taste better," Lydia explained. "Dad has tried some other hardneck varieties, like Russian and Music, but he always goes back to the German. It grows well here, despite the clay soil, and it's been very reliable."

Erin was laying out lengths of twine along the row of plants and Lydia explained that they bundled ten plants together, tied the bundle midway along the plant so it would hang straight, and then each bundle was loaded onto the wagon. The bulbs had to be put into the shade or they would start to cook in the sun.

As he bent to pull his first bulb, Dan noticed that each row was actually three plants wide and the plants were surrounded by wool. Lydia was on the opposite side of the row and had started pulling, cleaning, and dropping the plants into piles. Dan quickly got into the rhythm of the motions involved but he was still falling farther behind Lydia in the row. Lydia made it look effortless and he stood upright just to watch her for a minute. Eric was moving along next to her, pulling the middle bulb from the row of three.

Each row looked about a hundred feet long and Lydia reached the end and straightened her back. She and Eric started tying the bundles from that end and by the time Dan finished his row, they were tying the bundles he had made. He groaned out loud as he straightened his back and Lydia came up behind him and dug her thumbs into the muscles along his spine. "Too soon to be groaning; there are another two thousand bulbs to pull today." She knuckled his back muscles again and then removed her hands, moving away to the next row.

The twins had started pulling bulbs and Lydia pointed at the lengths of sisal twine laid next to the row. "If you could tie bundles for this row, Dan, I'll trade jobs with you for the next," she said, smiling at him. "When the wagon is full, we'll take a break while we move it over to the drying shed. You okay with this?" she asked.

"Hey, I was just hitting my stride. I'll pull. You bundle."

Lydia shook her head. "We'll all pull, so come on. Start at this end and I'll meet you in the middle. See if you can keep up with me, Ace." She laughed, moving toward the far end of the row.

The wagon quickly filled with tied bundles and Lydia called a halt. Lydia pulled Dan to the back of the wagon and hopped onto the end with her legs dangling off and Dan hitched his hip onto the edge just as Eric put the tractor in gear. Lydia grabbed his arm to steady him. His skin was slick with sweat and Lydia watched him pull his cap off and wipe his face with it.

When the wagon stopped in the shade of a tall building, Lydia hopped off and grabbed the end of a hose. With a quick yank on the handle of a hydrant, water gushed out. Lydia dropped her hat to the ground and stuck her head into the flow of water, letting it soak her head and run down her back and chest. Suddenly, Dan was just as wet, as she pointed the water directly at him and laughed. Eric grabbed the hose from her, soaked himself, and then caught Erin with the stream of water as she walked around the end of the wagon. Erin shrieked and Dan laughed until she grabbed the hose from her brother and blasted him with the spray.

He couldn't remember the last time he had enjoyed a water fight and laughed again. Eric shook himself like a dog and shut off the water. They sat in the shade, drinking water from the bottles in the cooler until

Lydia reminded them that they were only half done pulling for the day. And they needed to get this lot inside and hung, then had to be at Irv's at four o'clock to milk.

"And here I thought this pastoral life was all about lying in the shade in a hammock and sipping iced tea all summer. Nobody told me it was work," Dan groused, rolling to his feet and then reaching a hand to Lydia and Erin to pull them to their feet. "I think I've been conned."

"I distinctly remember that you volunteered for this duty, Ace," Lydia retorted, brushing the seat of her jeans and watching the dimple appear in his cheek. Man, he was cute when he did that. Not that she paid attention to such things, of course. This was scientific work she was engaged in, after all. But when he leaned over and kissed her nose, she forgot what she was doing for a minute. Work, for heaven's sake. That was it. There was work to do.

Dan turned away, reaching for the bundles of garlic that Eric had moved to the tailgate of the wagon, grabbing the trailing ends of sisal twine and wrapping them around his hand. With a half-dozen bundles dangling form each fist, he followed Eric into the shed where Erin was already hanging bundles from galvanized poles stretching the width of the barn.

He put his burden down on the concrete floor next to Eric's and turned around and bumped into Lydia. He grabbed her arms and murmured "Good excuse" before kissing her squarely on the lips and then walking away.

She was so surprised she stood there for a second before turning around to watch him walk outside. Erin was pretending to be oblivious, looking the other way but grinning widely when Lydia turned around again. Now she was hot all over again. She needed to soak her head again for sure! If she wasn't careful, she was going to lose it and not find it again anytime soon.

The inside of the shed was still fairly cool and Eric had turned on the big exhaust fans to keep the air circulating. By the time they made the trip to the shed with the last load, the outside temperature had risen to an uncomfortable level and they all were hot and tired. When she had hung the last bundle, Lydia walked outside, turned on the hydrant, and pointed the hose skyward. The water shot upward and then cascaded down on top of her head, soaking her hair and her clothes. "Aaaahhhhhhhh." She had her eyes closed when she felt a body next to her and opened them to see Dan and then Erin and Eric join her under the spray. They stood there for a minute and then Lydia began to laugh. Erin was giggling and Dan began singing a ditty about sailing the ocean in a hurricane. It made Eric laugh so hard he bent over, choking. Erin slapped him on the back and he fell over onto the grass at their feet. He lay there on his back, letting the water rain down on him, still laughing.

Erin reached to turn the hydrant off and they all stood there and looked at each other, dripping onto Eric.

"Nice work, everybody. I've put my whip away for the day, so let's go eat." Lydia looked at Dan and he quickly said, "I've got to change."

"I don't know. You look kinda cute that way," Lydia said.

He laughed before he started toward the cottage and Lydia stood there admiring the way wet denim adhered to long legs and a tight rear end until Erin poked her in the side. "No drooling allowed, Auntie," she admonished, grinning widely.

Lydia whipped her head around to look at Erin. "No grinning allowed, Niece." With a raised eyebrow, she said, "One should be aware of one's surroundings, that's all."

"Right." Erin hooked her arm through Lydia's and urged her toward the house. "You want tuna sandwiches for lunch?"

"Uh, sure."

"I really like him," Erin said casually.

"Do you? He's too old for you," Lydia said.

"Don't start with that diversion stuff. I know what I know," she said, lowering her voice in an attempt to sound mysterious.

Lydia just smiled at her, nudging her with her shoulder. "No comment."

A quick, cool shower and clean clothes made them

all feel more human and they were in the kitchen, putting together tuna sandwiches when Dan tapped on the kitchen door frame. Erin handed him a platter of sandwiches and a bag of chips with instructions to lay it out on the table. By the time he had set it down, Eric was there with big paper cups filled with ice, paper plates, and napkins. Erin had sliced cherry tomatoes and the little red discs covered a plate she had in one hand, while she balanced a bowl of macaroni salad on her other arm. Eric grabbed the pitcher of iced tea from Lydia as she came out on the porch and she turned back to pick up a handful of utensils.

It was quiet for a couple of minutes as they ate and gulped quantities of tea.

Eric finally sat back and belched, a long rambling sound that made everyone else stop and look at him. He smiled angelically and patted his stomach.

"Very nice, Eric." Lydia laughed. "Does your mother let you get away with that?"

"Sure. Our Irish cousins are worse, right, Erin?" He turned his head to see Erin eyeing him with revulsion. "You are *so* disgusting." She shuddered.

"You just think so because you can't do it," Eric retorted.

Erin huffed and started to say something, but Lydia cut her off, saying, "Enough, children. Eric, you are gross," she said, smiling at him, "and Erin, you're right. Now go away for a while."

While they cleared the table, she looked at Dan to

see him winking at Eric. "What?" she asked him. "And don't tell me it's a guy thing."

He laughed out loud. "Actually, my sister had a whole repertoire of belches that she practiced. She used to entertain everybody at the dinner table until one time she did it in front of some guy she had a crush on."

"I get it. He didn't think it was funny, huh?" Lydia grinned at him, leaning back in her chair.

"Nope. And that worked better than all the nagging my mom had done, trying to get her to stop."

"We have to be at Irv's at four," Lydia called after the twins as they left the kitchen. She looked at Dan. "Maybe we'll go to the movies tonight. Want to come?"

He shook his head. "I've got a bunch of stuff to catch up on and I've been neglecting the book too much. I'd better get on it. Editors don't like it much when they get behind deadline." He looked at her again. "What's up now?"

"Now is when we do that hammock and iced tea thing you mentioned. Since we don't have a hammock, I plan to just veg out right where I am, maybe read a book that has no socially redeeming value and not think about garlic for a couple of hours. What do you think?"

"I think I'd like to do that. You want company?"

"Yours? Yes." Lydia studied his face, seeing the lines at the corners of his dark brown eyes deepen, even though his mouth wasn't really smiling, just softening slightly as he leaned toward her.

He took a breath. "Good. I'll go get my laptop. Maybe I can get something done on the book." He wasn't sure he could, knowing that he would be distracted by being in the same space with Lydia, but he could try. "Come with me," he said, rising to his feet and reaching for her hand.

They tried to stay in the shade from overhanging branches as they walked slowly down the lane leading from the house. With her fingers twined in his, Lydia resisted the urge to lean into him and asked, "How's your investigation going? Or can you not tell me anything more than I already know?"

He glanced down at her, pulling her closer to him. "Nothing more. We're on hold."

"You sound annoyed."

"Yeah," he said. "I'm not real good at waiting, although you'd think I would be by now. There's a lot of it in this business. Waiting for information, waiting for something to happen, waiting for the right people to show up, waiting for suspects to show their hand—you know, waiting and hoping you're ready when it goes down."

"You've been at it a long time?" she remarked, a question in her voice.

"Ten years now. I was recruited out of college, and truthfully, I've loved the work. I was never interested in the military and DEA was a good choice for me. I joined the Mobile Enforcement Team project and I've been around the country with a team ever since."

"But you live in Annapolis, right?"

"Sure, when I'm home, but we frequently get called in to another jurisdiction when the investigation is big enough and they need more manpower in the field, like this one. So, since I've been part of a Mobile Enforcement Team, I've never stayed in one place for long." He looked at her, seeing a frown form on her face.

"Are the local law enforcement people in on this?" she asked.

"They're the reason DEA is here. The Sheriff's Department requested it." He nodded. "Your friend Butch must have been out of the loop, but I bet he's been asking questions around the department and is on to it by now." He laughed.

After a moment, she glanced at him. "Uncle Mark was in for thirty years, you know, so we all kind of know what you people do." She paused, looking at him. "Are you ever going to tell me how you got that scar on your back? Is it from a bullet wound?"

His fingers tightened on hers for a second. "Yeah."

She cocked an eyebrow at him, wanting to know more. "And?"

"And it was just a ricochet. You know," he said, "not a direct hit. Tore up the flesh a bit but didn't hit anything vital. Hurt like hell, though," he admitted.

"How old were you?" Lydia studied his face, very aware of his fingers wrapped around hers.

"Twenty-five. A hotshot kid," he admitted.

"You got over that, I bet. I mean the hotshot part." She was relieved when he laughed.

"It was an instantaneous conversion, let me tell you." He grimaced at the memory. "A glimpse at your own mortality can convert you quicker than anything else, I guess. It certainly made me more careful."

He shrugged slightly, pushing away the memory of that night. "And I'm ready to get out now." He looked down at her, pulling her tight against his side. "I've got some other things I want to do now."

Lydia tried hard not to get all warm and cozy at his words. He could be talking about his writing, starting a new book, making a living with his writing, staying in one place instead of moving wherever the job took him. Any of those, she told herself. But Dan was still looking at her and now even his eyes were smiling at her, inviting her to accept his meaning. It wasn't about writing or getting tired of the job; it was about her.

When she didn't say anything, he stopped walking, swinging her around up against his chest and holding her there with his hands at her waist. "I like it here. I like the river. I like the farm. I like everything you do. I like your relatives. I more than like you."

"Uh, Dan? You've only been here a short time. You've only known me for, let's see, nine days. Maybe you'll change your mind, find something you like more." God, she hoped not!

"Nope, I won't. I know exactly what I want," he whispered just before he kissed her.

His mouth was warm on hers; in fact, it was starting to feel really hot, she thought, as she closed her eyes and leaned into him. It could have been seconds or minutes before he pulled his lips away from hers, then ran them along her jaw to her ear. The little nip on her earlobe made her open her eyes and she realized that her arms were around his neck and she was holding on tight. His hands were moving up and down her back as she eased her arms down and stepped back a few inches.

"Maybe I do too," she said softly, watching his dimple appear as he smiled.

Chapter Fifteen

Lydia sat on the swing on the porch of the cottage while Dan went inside to gather his laptop and the briefcase containing the manuscript and his notes. The cottage looked over the pond, the old apple orchard, and some of the pastures. It had a view of some hay fields showing the dense green of new growth and Lydia thought it was the prettiest sight in the world.

She heard the squeak of the screen door and got to her feet as Dan came out the door, carrying a leather case in one hand. He reached for her with his other hand and let the door bang shut behind him. "I'm determined to get this rewrite done, so let's go," he said, pulling her behind him down the steps. "I'm facing a deadline here."

"Okay. You write and I'll read. In fact, you don't

need to come with me to Irv's this afternoon. The twins will help and you could keep working."

"No way. You need me," he insisted.

Lydia thought that might be true and she wasn't thinking just about milking Irv's cows.

While Dan got his computer set up at the big table on the screened porch, Lydia went to find Eric, thinking that a night at the movies would break up the daily workload. Eric looked up from the book he was reading when Lydia tapped on his door.

"A movie? Yeah, great. Where's Erin?"

"In her room, I think. I'm just going there to ask her. We can go after chores. Check the paper and figure out the time, will you? I'm going to call Sophie at the bookstore and see if she wants to go with us," she said, turning away and starting down the hallway. There was a multiplex theater in the village so finding something to see shouldn't be too hard.

With a book that she had retrieved from her bedside table tucked under her arm, she stuck her head in Erin's room to find her crawling around the floor, pinning the backing to a quilt that Lydia's own mother had been working on. "Need help with that, Erin?

"Uh-uh," she said. "I'm done. Did I hear you say something about the movies?"

Lydia grinned at her. "I thought it would be good to get out of here for a couple of hours. Okay with you?"

"You bet. Eric and I can do the chores and check the sheep as soon as we get back from Irv's. Maybe we could go to Frazier's for supper afterward," she added hopefully.

"You convinced me," Lydia agreed, tucking her book more securely under her arm. "We haven't been there in weeks."

Dan was hunched over his computer when Lydia returned to the kitchen, intent on getting a glass of iced tea. She didn't bother disturbing him, just filled a glass for him, stirred in a couple of spoons of sugar, and splashed in a big dose of lemon juice, knowing he liked it that way. When she set it down away from the papers he had scattered on the table, he looked up long enough to smile and then returned his attention to the computer screen.

Lydia stretched her legs out on the settee and leaned her back against the arm, setting her glass on the floor next to her. She was very aware of Dan sitting a few feet away from her and she stopped reading to watch him. His concentration was intense as he focused on the pages of manuscript slowly scrolling on the computer screen. Occasionally, he would stop and correct a word or reach for the papers stacked on the table, pulling one from the pile and reading through it before returning to the computer.

The only sound outside the porch was the faint but distinct whirring of cicadas. The birds were silent in the heat of the afternoon and the sheep and cows were out in the far fields, too distant to hear and probably all resting quietly in the shade.

The hum of Dan's computer was like a white noise to Lydia and she closed the book and tucked it next to her. Her mind shut down and her body relaxed into the cushions.

She was startled awake when the refrigerator door slammed and opened her eyes to see Dan looking at her from under his half-closed eyelids. He was sprawled in one of the wicker chairs, his feet up on the ottoman. She rolled to her side and sat up, rubbing her face before she looked at her watch. Almost four o'clock. Dan's computer was closed and unplugged, and she flushed a little, knowing he had been watching her sleep. *I hope I didn't snore,* she thought.

Erin came out onto the porch, tipping a bottle of water to her mouth. "You guys ready to rock and roll?"

"Sure. Just give me a minute to wash my face. I was asleep, I think. I hate to sleep in the afternoon," she grumbled. "I always feel half-dead when I wake up."

Dan grinned at her, sitting up in his chair and letting his feet fall to the floor. "You were only out for a half hour, I think." He raised his eyebrows at her. "Pick me up at the cottage?"

"Right," Erin answered for her as Lydia left the porch. "She's embarrassed 'cause she fell asleep and you were probably watching her, weren't you?" she questioned.

"Guilty." He shrugged. "Doing the Sleeping Beauty fantasy, you know?" he said, picking up the computer and sliding it into the briefcase, and then tucking it under his arm. "My intentions are honorable, Erin. Don't worry."

"Oh, I'm not worried, Dan," she admitted. "She can handle you. You'd better hurry," she advised, "or you'll miss the bus."

Dan grinned at her, opening the porch door and jumping to the bottom of the steps.

Irving wasn't around when they started the milking routine that afternoon. Fred was pushing the silage cart and Dan relieved him of it, gently slapping him on the back and asking Fred if he minded letting him take over. Fred coughed and shook his head, looking grateful for the help. He stopped by Lydia as she filled the teat dip dispenser and jerked his head toward Dan. "Nice young man you got there, Lydia. Your daddy and momma like him?"

Lydia could feel herself blushing. "Since when did you become a matchmaker, Fred?"

His wide grin showed his few remaining teeth, stained yellow from tobacco and rotten from neglect. Not a pretty sight. But she had known him since she was a child and his state of health and hygiene didn't surprise her. He had worked for Irv long before she was in high school and was coming to this farm twice a day to help with the milking. Fred had always been polite to her, helpful when he could be, and reliable. She could see that he was failing more, weaker and more short of breath than last summer and she wondered if Irv would let him continue to live in the trailer on the farm that he and his wife had occupied, even when he could no longer work.

She shook her head at him. "Dad and Mom are still away." She glanced out the door at the cows waiting at the gate. Eric was walking toward them, ready to let them into the stanchions.

The lowing of the cows drowned out every other sound for a few minutes while the animals sought out their usual positions, and then Lydia could hear the clanging of metal as the stanchion head catches were closed, one at a time.

She looked at Fred, noting the pinched look of his face and the rapid heaving of his chest. "Go outside for a while, Fred. We'll do all this. The dust in here can't be good for you."

"I know it ain't, Lydia. I'll do what you say," he said, then leaned over to cough and spit into the gutter.

Lydia patted him on the back and tried to ignore the rattle in his chest as he coughed again.

Dan was walking toward her, his eyes on Fred, and he took the old man's arm and gently pulled him toward the door and around the corner into the shade.

Lydia moved toward the first cow in line. Dan came back a minute later and stayed just ahead of her, cleaning the udder of the next cow. She thought he looked like a natural: gentle, reassuring, moving calmly from animal to animal. He had mastered the position to stop a kick before it gained any force. He had handled Fred the same way—gentle, reassuring, calm.

As she automatically attached teat cups, checked for milk-out and dipped teats, she mused on the contrast with the way he lived his regular life, always looking for danger, probably cynical, suspicious, maybe even deadly when necessary. How hard would it be for him to abandon that for a life that might be more settled but could be boring? Not a question she could answer and she left off thinking about it when she heard Irv's voice boom through the barn.

The cows immediately went on alert, looking around for the source of the noise, and then relaxed again, resuming their search for the tastiest morsel and trying to reach a neighbor's portion to steal what they could. It wasn't right to anthropomorphize cows but the similarity to human behavior had certainly struck her many times in the past. Greed, anger, hate, lust, un-kindness, the worst of human traits, as well as the best, were apparent every day in a barnyard or field. Scary stuff, she thought, straightening up as Irv stopped be-hind her.

"Hey, Irving," she greeted him. "What's new? Any word on Billy?"

"Damn fool. They're letting him out of the hospital, Kay said. They called her to come get him. Jaw wasn't really broken so they didn't wire it shut. Should have," he continued. "Now I'll have to listen to him whine."

Lydia laughed. "Billy has always been good at whining, Irving."

"Yeah, and now he'll be useless as a pink skirt on a boar hog," Irv complained.

Lydia could see Dan laugh as he caught that comment and then she listened to a litany of complaints about Irv's help. Not one of them was worth the time it took him to write their paychecks and he was ready to fire the lot of them. His dairyman had gotten himself arrested, his field man had gotten beat up, and poor Fred was useless, he groused.

Lydia nodded and milked his cows. It wasn't any use offering advice, or even a comment, when Irv was on a rant. Or any other time, for that matter, she reflected. Irving had learned the dairy business from his father, who the locals said was the tightest man in the county. And Irv had put his father on a pedestal, quoting the gospel according to Irving Senior. Pointing out to him that hiring one good worker and paying a living wage would be better than paying three bad workers at minimum wage was a waste of breath.

Irv continued to complain and Lydia continued to milk cows and Dan listened with an expression on his face that approached disbelief.

By the time they got to the end of the aisle, Irving had veered off onto the topic of his clever deals, buying and selling cattle, and Lydia stopped listening. She had heard these stories too many times already. Dan was looking a little shell-shocked, she thought, glancing at him as she straightened up from the last cow. She winked at him and watched his dimple appear. Irv was oblivious, still telling his stories, when she walked back down the aisle and shut off the motors.

The loss of that background hum made Irv's voice seem even louder. The cows continued to chew, their jaws grinding from side to side, and a few of them looked around, as if they were listening to the stories. Lydia suspected they had heard them all before, since Irv tended to relate them to any visitor who tarried long enough to get caught in the stream of words flowing from his mouth. His wife was the only one Lydia knew who could shut him off, and she did it with a look.

Lydia grabbed Dan by the hand and pulled him toward the door, waving to Irving as she left, promising him they would be back in the morning. The twins caught up with them, assuring her that the calves were fed. Fred was still sitting in the shade as they passed the corner of the barn. He had a cigarette dangling from his mouth and he lifted a hand to wave at her. Lydia returned the gesture, calling a good-bye as she dragged Dan toward the SUV.

He was laughing as he opened the door for her. "An interesting character. You planning to write a book featuring his stories?"

She groaned as she climbed into her seat. "I'll leave that to you, I think. I've been listening to those same stories for years and by now, I don't know which ones are true and which ones he makes up," she commented as she closed the door.

Minutes later, she pulled behind the house and turned to look at Erin and Eric. "You guys get the chores done, will you? I'll drop Dan off at the cottage."

After they had scrambled out of the backseat, she put the SUV in gear and took the lane leading to the cottage. Dan looked at her, smiling. "You saw me talking to Fred and want to know everything, right?"

"Well, of course. I just didn't want to put the screws to you in front of the twins."

She shut off the engine after she stopped in front of the cottage and turned toward him.

"He's a pretty sick old guy, isn't he?" Dan shook his head. "And still smokes."

"He's been in bad shape for a long time," Lydia assured him. "Don't try to distract me here."

He unfastened his seat belt, turned, and pulled her toward him, sliding a hand to the back of her head and bringing his lips to the corner of her mouth. "Not even this kind of distraction?"

"Um, maybe," she said, turning her head so their lips met with the lightest touch. She felt his tongue slide along her bottom lip and shivered.

Dan pulled back, enjoying the dazed look on her face and then said, "You know his daughter is Robert's wife, I expect." At her nod, he went on. "According to Fred, they all knew about Billy's little foray into the drug business. His kid was selling it at the high school and

Robert got jealous and wanted a piece of the action. So he beat up Billy, intending to take his place as the pickup guy and help himself to more of the stuff. He told his wife that Billy was a fool for not helping himself to a bigger share and he bragged that he was smart enough to get away with it by adding sugar to the packets so nobody would notice." He rolled his eyes. "Yeah, like these guys wouldn't notice. Robert was going to get himself dead in a hurry."

"What about Billy?"

"He's so scared right now it wasn't hard to get his cooperation. Kevin is very good at twisting arms." He grinned. He leaned over and kissed her again before opening his door and sliding out. "See you later."

Chapter Sixteen

There were six movies to choose from and Lydia found herself alone at the back of one of the theaters. She was slumped down in the seat, watching the ads flash on the screen when the seat next to her squeaked. Her friend Sophie grinned at her, then reached into her backpack and pulled out a big bag of M&Ms. Lydia kept her eyes on the bag, ignoring the screen and making smacking noises with her lips. "Be quiet, Lydia. You want to get me busted?"

Lydia snickered softly, knowing that nobody was going to throw them out for bringing M&Ms into the theater illicitly. Sophie's younger sister was dating the son of the owner of the place, the heir apparent to the local theater empire. Lydia watched as Sophie looked around before quietly opening the bag and then bringing a plastic bag from her pocket and pouring a generous pile of candy into it.

"I'm glad you dragged yourself away from the books long enough to come to the movies, Soph. I was afraid you only read books, now that you own the bookstore."

"Not likely. I've seen every movie that's come through here," she whispered, passing over the plastic bag. "Where are the kids?"

"Next door, watching some action flick. You want to go to Frazier's with us later?"

"Definitely." She closed her mouth and looked apologetically at the woman in front of them who had turned around at their whispering. "Sorry," she mouthed and looked up at the screen.

They got up to leave as the credits started scrolling on the screen and spotted Erin waiting at the exit. It was still light outside and they found Eric in the parking lot, leaning against the side of the SUV.

"I guess I don't have to ask you if you're hungry, do I?" Lydia asked as they approached him. "We'll meet you there, okay, Sophie?"

Sophie nodded and greeted Eric with a grin before she angled off to find her own car, parked on the other side of the lot.

Frazier's was crowded, with a line snaking from the bar to the entrance, when Eric pulled open the door. Sophie grinned at them from the end of the line.

"It's moving pretty fast, so come on in. It's pretty busy for the middle of the week."

Lydia leaned against the wall, surveying the people ahead of them. "The tourists have discovered the place, I guess."

"I know," Sophie agreed, "and the food is great."

"No argument there," Lydia said as they moved forward toward the front of the line. "What are you staring at?" she asked, bringing her friend's attention back from her intense stare into the bar area.

Just then, the man in front of her stepped forward, following a waitress waving a menu. Lydia looked directly into the bar room as Sophie mumbled in her ear. "See the blond guy at the bar? He's been in the bookstore a couple of times. He is *so* hot." She sighed.

Lydia looked in the direction Sophie indicated and recognized the blond man staring at the TV screen above the bar. Dan was cradling a glass of beer between his hands, sitting on the stool next to him. His eyes found Lydia and he smiled at her before letting his gaze move on to notice Erin and Eric standing behind her. His friend glanced their way and said something to Dan before returning his attention to the screen.

A minute later, Lydia and Sophie, trailed by the twins, were following a waitress to the back of the room and being seated at a long table against the back wall. Sophie nudged her and Lydia looked up to see the two men walking toward them. Sophie had a big smile on her face as Dan greeted them. She pulled out the chair next to her and Lydia swore that she batted her eyelashes at the blond and gave him a "come hither" look. She looked across at her friend's expression of satisfaction as her target settled into the chair next to her.

Dan's hand was on Lydia's shoulder as he leaned close to her ear. "I hope you don't mind if we join you, because I think we already did," he said, grinning at his friend across the table. He sat down next to Lydia, his shoulder touching hers as he greeted the twins and introduced his friend. Sophie returned his greeting but her attention was on Kevin and Lydia rolled her eyes, poking Dan in the ribs.

"Look out now, it's getting hot in here," she whispered out of the side of her mouth. "Sophie's on a mission. She'll have all his secrets out of him before he realizes it."

"I don't think so," Dan responded. "He's the most closemouthed guy I've ever known."

The waitress came to take their orders and when she left, Lydia turned her attention to Kevin. His skin was tanned and his blond good looks and preppy clothes screamed Ivy League, yacht club, money. Nobody seeing him would think "Drug Enforcement Agency hotshot." It was a great cover, Lydia thought. She eyed Sophie, who was laughing at something Kevin said, and sighed.

Dan was talking to Erin but turned to look at her. "Kevin's one of the good guys. Don't worry," he said, glancing at his friend and Sophie.

"I know. She can take care of herself," Lydia said.

"Yeah," Dan answered, looking across the table as Kevin bent his head toward Sophie and said something in her ear. "I hope Kevin can," he added, lowering one eyelid at her in a brief wink.

On the way out of the restaurant an hour later, Lydia felt Dan hesitate and saw him glance sideways toward one of the booths at the back of the bar room. His hand was against her back or she wouldn't have noticed the change in attention or the tightening of his fingers. When she looked around, he stepped to her side, blocking her view and propelling her toward the exit. She and Sophie were walking down the street before she realized that he had dropped farther back and was talking intently to Kevin. Sophie looked back at them and then looked a question at Lydia.

Lydia shrugged and kept walking. By the time they reached Sophie's car, Dan and Kevin had caught up with them. Lydia waved at Sophie as she pulled away and Dan caught her other hand, walking toward the SUV.

The two men were standing on the sidewalk talking when Lydia pulled away from the curb. The rearview mirror showed them walking back toward Frazier's, and just as the light at the intersection turned green, she saw them duck back into the restaurant.

"Okay, how do you want to handle this?" Kevin asked as he and Dan went through the front door of Frazier's. "You're sure it's the guy from the pickup vehicle?"

Dan nodded. "Head for the bar. He's sitting in a booth at the back of the bar room. There's somebody with him and I'd sure like to get a look at whoever that is."

The mirror behind the bar reflected the dim interior of the room. Straddling a stool, Dan looked up at the TV, then let his eyes flick to the mirror. He and Kevin stared up at the TV, pretending a deep interest in the baseball game. Somebody hit a double and noise erupted from the far end of the bar. While the din continued, Dan told Kevin to check the table by the emergency exit. There was enough light from the overhead exit sign to show the face of a beefy guy in a sport jacket talking to a smaller man seated across from him.

Dan sipped his beer, watching the TV screen while Kevin studied the two seated by the exit. "That's our guy. I don't think much of his wardrobe," he said, his voice barely audible above the noise from the TV and the baseball crowd. "That's the same ugly jacket he was wearing when you got him on film."

"Yeah," Dan said. "Can you see the other guy?"

"Yup. I'll be darned, 'cause I know who he is. I've seen a picture of that mug." He paused and then muttered, "Get out on the street. They're getting ready to leave." Dan glanced in the mirror and saw both men standing up, dropping money on the table.

He slid from the stool and slapped Kevin on the back. He sauntered toward the front and went out the exit, crossed the street, and waited in the shadows between streetlights.

A couple of minutes passed while Dan checked the street. A couple walked past him, kissing and groping each other, totally oblivious to him. Three white-haired ladies came through the exit door and then walked away, talking and giggling.

Sport Jacket and his buddy finally came out and walked north along the sidewalk, stopping at a dark blue Mercedes. He could see them talking but was too far away to hear even the murmur of voices. The smaller man got in the driver's seat of the Mercedes, fired it up, and pulled away. The sport-coated figure get into an old Toyota parked in the next space.

He rummaged through his pockets again, found a pen, and wrote the Mercedes' plate number on his forearm. The Toyota passed him and he added that plate number to his forearm. He watched the Toyota turn the corner before he walked across the street and saw Kevin step out from the side of the building.

"So who's the little guy, Kev?"

"Sheldon Shitsky, a sleaze lawyer in the city. The Agency has been watching him, but up 'til now, hasn't been able to definitely tie him to this operation. The bosses are going to be very happy with you, son," he grinned, poking Dan in the ribs.

"Huh. Meet me at the cottage. We need to call this in."

They sat on the top step, looking at the reflection of the moon on the pond, listening to a hawk cry from the old orchard. "Nice girl, Lydia," Kevin commented. "You getting serious?"

"Yup," Dan answered, not elaborating.

Kevin stared at the moon. "I heard that you put in a letter of resignation. You really going to do it?"

"Yeah. What about you?"

Kevin leaned against the post, not saying anything. Then he leaned forward again, clasping his hands between his knees. "I think I'll take some vacation time. Maybe hang around here a while. The company's not bad."

"Sophie, huh?" Dan grinned, reaching for his phone as it vibrated against his hip. His expression was serious as he listened but when he disconnected, he looked at Kevin and he laughed.

"Man! You're good! Sheldon Shitsky, dirty lawyer. That Mercedes is leased to him and the description fits. The boss sends his thanks. They were able to get some financial stuff on him and this sighting tightens the noose. He's pretty sure they can get him now."

Kevin stood up, stretching his arms over his head. "Okay," he said with satisfaction. "I'm off to get some sleep. I've got a breakfast date in the morning."

"Nice," Dan commented. "We'll be milking cows at four A.M. and then harvesting garlic."

Kevin laughed. "Bucolic splendor, huh?"

"Something like that," Dan admitted, grinning.

When the taillights of Kevin's car disappeared, Dan rose to his feet. Four in the morning would come too soon. He thought about the people who rose before dawn every single day to milk cows, worked hard all day, milked those same cows again before allowing themselves to rest. Nobody would live like that unless they loved the life, the land, the animals. It certainly wasn't about money. It wasn't his life, but he admired those who did it.

Four o'clock did come too soon, but he was ready and waiting on the porch when Lydia pulled up and pushed the passenger door open. She watched as he fastened his seat belt before she handed him a travel mug and smiled. "Coffee sometimes helps," she said. He groaned softly and sipped from the mug.

Five minutes later, they had pulled into the yard next to the milking parlor. Lydia turned off the engine, undid her seat belt, and leaned against her door. The smell and taste of coffee was comforting and she sipped from her own mug. Dan looked sleepy and rumpled, his nose an inch from his mug, sniffing the steam rising from the lid.

"Not a morning person?"

"This isn't morning! This is the middle of the night," he said. "I've been on enough stakeouts to recognize morning when I see it." He looked at her out of the corner of his eye and saw her smiling at him and smiled himself. "You are some woman, Lydia."

"Hey, you won't see me doing this for much longer. Either Robert will be back, once Irv gets over his snit and bails him out, or he'll find somebody else permanent to replace him. And it won't be me," she assured him. "I like to loll around in bed 'til at least six o'clock in the summer."

Dan laughed and put his mug into the holder. "You ready to get this done?" he asked, opening his door and getting out. He came around the vehicle and had her door open before she had taken the last sip of coffee and tucked the mug into a holder.

When she stood up, he pressed a quick kiss to her mouth, then took her arm and held her close to his body as they walked past the cows waiting patiently at the gate. He released her as they went through the door and headed toward Fred who was struggling with the feed cart. The motors were running and Lydia saw Irv hooking the portable machine to a cow whose rear view told its story. She had calved recently and her udder was distended and dripping milk from the teats. She kicked at the hoses attached to the teat cups, but wasn't successful in dislodging the cups. Lydia knew that she would settle down in a minute as the pressure in her udder was relieved, and she turned in the other direction to begin the business of milking the main herd.

Fred went to let the herd into the barn, and after each cow was secured, she started the routine of washing the udder, attaching the cups, checking for milk-out, removing the teat cups, and dipping teats. Ten minutes later, Dan was there, prepping the cows for her, talking to each cow as he worked, touching them to let them know where he was, soothing a restless first calf heifer who objected to the whole business. He grinned at Lydia. "Not a morning cow, obviously."

Fortunately, Irv was busy feeding the calves and the milking went without interruption. Fred was outside, smoking a cigarette, when they left the barn. Lydia waved to him and Dan walked toward him and stopped to talk. Lydia heard a tractor start up and turned to see Billy backing the manure spreader up to the end of the barn. In the dim light coming from the open door, Billy's face looked swollen, his nose hidden by white tape. He didn't look around at them, concentrating on getting the spreader positioned under the end of the gutter cleaner.

Lydia walked quickly to the SUV and got inside before Dan caught up with her. She had the engine running when he climbed in and had started out toward the road before he had his seat belt fastened. She was laughing when she glanced at him. "Did you see Billy? He's back to work and looks like a freight train hit him in the face."

"Yeah, I know. Kevin talked to him and scared the crap out of him. I'd rather he didn't recognize me and tie me to you and the twins."

"Is Billy dangerous?"

"Probably not, but you know rats will fight if they're cornered." He yawned and looked toward her as they pulled in back of the farmhouse. "I am badly in need of a nap," he commented.

"That was going to be my line." Lydia laughed. "Come in and use the couch. I'll wake you up for breakfast."

They shucked their sneakers at the back door and Dan followed her through the house. He admired her back, slim and straight, and admired the way her jeans fit her legs and bottom. She started up the stairs and he watched until she turned around and started back down. She stopped on the bottom step, leaned toward him, and quickly kissed his mouth before turning around and walking back up the stairs.

"Hey," he called softly.

When she looked back down at him, he just stood there, smiling. After a few seconds, she walked away down the hall and he finally went into the living room and stretched out on the couch.

Chapter Seventeen

The sky was clouded over when they finished hanging the last bundle of garlic. The temperature had dropped ten degrees and the wind was gusting hard enough to make the American flag stand straight out from its pole next to the hay barn.

Eric looked at the sky, then at Erin and said, "Lunch." He started toward the house with Erin hurrying to catch up. Lydia stood in the doorway of the shed, watching the clouds. She felt Dan come to stand next to her and turned her head to look at him. "Thunderstorms this afternoon. I'll bet the kids will want to play basketball."

Dan raised his eyebrow and she answered his unspoken question. "There's a hoop in the machinery shed.

We just move the tractor out into the yard and play on the concrete floor in there. Hard on your knees and hands if you fall," she admitted, grinning at him. "You up for it? You should know that we take no prisoners."

"Me neither." His eyes were on her mouth and he watched her swallow and then lick her lips. "I'm ready when you are," he added, watching the color slide up her neck.

Lydia didn't respond, just started walking toward the farmhouse. After she had gone a hundred feet, she reached for his hand, sliding her fingers between his. She didn't say anything and he looked down at her profile, noticing that her lips were turned up in a slight smile.

By the time they reached the house, Erin was cooking hot dogs and Eric was sprawled on the wicker settee on the porch, flipping through a magazine. Thunder rumbled in the distance and rain started to spit down, blowing in through the screens.

Lydia carried plates and glasses into the dining room and flipped on the lights. Erin pulled open the oven door and the smell of hot potato knishes competed with the smell of hot dogs. Erin called it her New York lunch when she brought everything to the table—Coney Island wieners, potato knishes, dill pickles, and chips.

There was a flash of lightning and the rain suddenly fell in sheets, slashing against the windows. A loud clap of thunder followed and the lights dimmed for a split second and Dan glanced over at Lydia. She grinned at him. "Good thing we got all the garlic harvested. You would not have enjoyed pulling soggy plants."

When Eric reached for his fourth hot dog, Erin snickered. "We are so going to whip your butt today. The load of food you put away is going to weigh you down so you won't be able to get your feet off the ground if you try a lay-up."

"You'd like to think so, but I'm merely fueling up. You playing, Dan?" Eric asked, turning his attention away from his sister. When Dan nodded, grinning, Eric looked at his sister triumphantly. "We're gonna wipe the floor with you."

Erin snorted and Lydia laughed out loud. "Okay. We meet one hour from now in the machinery shed. No-holds-barred, winner takes all." Lydia looked at Dan, thinking that he hadn't heard her. He looked abstracted and she touched his arm.

He looked at her, shaking his head slightly before he smiled. "Just thinking about something else. Sorry. I'll go work on my book and see you in an hour," he said. He helped clear the table, then left the house without saying anything else. He had been thinking about a family of his own, children of his own, and Lydia, sitting around the table, teasing and laughing, and he wanted it all.

The repetitive thumping sound broke his concentration and Dan looked up from his laptop just as he heard a shout. He had had a hard time dragging his thoughts back to the manuscript in front of him. Now he pushed his chair away from the desk and went outside to stand on the porch. He could hear the sound of voices calling out and an occasional burst of laughter. The rain had settled down to a steady drizzle and the heavy air seemed to carry the sound in his direction. He glanced at his watch and realized that more than an hour had passed and he was late for the basketball match.

He exchanged his shorts for jeans, remembering the sting of concrete burns he had gotten as a kid. No point in changing his shirt. He was going out there to sweat some more, anyway.

There was a two-on-one game in progress when he got to the machinery shed and Eric was braving the onslaught of two determined females, guarding the net from Erin's drive toward the basket. He greeted Dan with a cry of joy, bending over with his hands on his knees. "They're killing me," he complained, taking in several huge breaths.

Dan assumed an evil grin and took up a position inside the key.

"Uh-oh. He looks like he knows what he's doing," Lydia mumbled to Erin. "We may be in trouble here."

An hour later, they were all collapsed on the concrete floor, dripping sweat and exhausted. Dan rolled his head to the side to look at Lydia, sprawled on her stomach a few feet away.

"I'm sure glad it doesn't rain every day if this is what you do whenever it does." He groaned softly. "I'm dying here."

He heard an "Umph" sound from Lydia and grinned as he sat up. "You guys are formidable," he congratulated the twins, getting to his feet and walking toward Lydia. He nudged her with the toe of his sneaker and heard her say, "Go away."

"No way, champ. Get up," he urged, leaning over to tug on her ponytail.

She rolled to her back, taking a deep breath. He grinned at her, reaching his hands down toward her. She looked at them suspiciously, and then up into his face. "Come on, give me your hands. I won't let you go," he assured her.

"Okay, we do need to get going if we're going to get to Irv's on time," she agreed as she grabbed his hands and let him pull her to her feet.

Lydia stepped outside through the side door of the building. Dan followed, pulling the door closed behind him. "I'm going to take a shower before we go to Irv's. I'm pretty sure I stink," he said.

Lydia nodded. "Me too," she said, pulling her shirt away from her skin. The drizzle had escalated to a steady rain and she tipped her head back to let the water fall on her face. "That was fun, though. We'll pick you up. Maybe Irv found somebody else to do the milking," she said hopefully.

"How hard is he trying?"

Lydia grinned at him. "As long as we're doing it? Probably not very hard," she admitted. "I'll talk to him, though. I've got a lot of work to do with the garlic. We start trimming and cleaning tomorrow and that takes a lot of time."

The rain was soaking both of them and Lydia pushed the wet hair out of her eyes. She looked at Dan, who was soaked to the skin, his jeans clinging to his legs. She looked down at herself and started to laugh. "No offense, but we both look awful. I'm going to the house," she said, turning away from him. "We'll pick you up," she repeated over her shoulder.

Dan jogged back to the cottage, mentally reliving the feel of Lydia's body against his when they had collided under the basket. He had wrapped his arms around her to keep her from falling and then had to talk himself into letting her go. Lydia had stood still for a minute, looking at him, before she turned away, grabbed the ball, and passed it off to Erin.

He stood under the shower for a couple of minutes, trying not to think too much about Lydia. By the time he had scrubbed down and washed his hair, the water was cooling off and so was he. He pulled on a pair of worn running shorts and was wrestling a T-shirt over his head when he walked out of the bathroom.

Kevin was sitting on the kitchen counter, grinning at him, holding an open can of soda in his hand. "Good thing I'm not the big bad wolf. Security on this place really sucks," he commented before chugging from the can.

"There's never been a need for security until you showed up, Kev. I'm willing to bet everybody leaves their door unlocked around here." Dan grabbed a can of soda from the refrigerator and sat in the desk chair.

"Not worried about biosecurity and terrorists?"

Dan shook his head. "This is a small community. They had *you* made in less than a day. Lydia had already figured out what was going on at the airport before I ever got here. Irv knew what his men were up to without one of us telling him." He paused, thinking. "Too bad he didn't stop it, of course, but now that I know him, it's pretty much what I'd expect from him."

He swallowed the rest of the soda and placed the can on the desk behind him. "Biosecurity is a problem with so few people watching the place but this is a small operation, not a likely target.

Kevin looked at him, shaking his head. "You really are getting indoctrinated. Here I thought you were a city boy. If I hear you playing country-western music on the radio, I'm leaving town, I swear." He laughed.

"Maybe a little Alan Jackson," he admitted, laughing when Kevin cocked an eyebrow at him. "What are you doing here, anyway? Something changed?"

"The boss wants us to keep an eye on the delivery

tonight. He doesn't expect anything. Just wants to cover the bases."

"Billy's out of the hospital. He was at Irv's this morning," Dan told him, adding that he looked pretty beaten up.

"Yeah, well, it could have been worse. That Robert is a mean son of a bitch. Billy's jaw wasn't really broken so they didn't have to wire it or he'd still be in the hospital." Kevin flashed a grin, adding, "I scared the bejesus out of him so he's cooperating and will do the pickup from the plane as usual. I'll be watching him so he doesn't try to screw up."

"You trust him?"

"Hell, no. But I'm pretty sure he's too stupid to figure out a way to warn them and too smart to try to do something I won't like. At this point, he's more scared of me than of Robert." Kevin shook his head. "Amazing gene pool around that place of Irv's."

Dan laughed out loud and got up, tossing his empty soda can toward the sink and listening to the clanking sound as it landed on target. "Okay, get out of here. I can see them coming to pick me up for the afternoon milking and you need to go play with Billy."

"Yeah. He's easy to follow, though. He has a distinctive scent: 'Eau de Billy Goat' I think it's called," he said as he went out the door. "See you at two."

Lydia pulled up next to Kevin's brown sedan and he leaned in her window, greeting her and the twins.

By the time Dan had pulled jeans over his shorts and grabbed his cap, Kevin was backing out the driveway.

Fred and Billy were in the barn when they got there and Billy was pushing the feed cart down the aisle. The cows were already stanchioned and Lydia sent Eric to get the standing milking machine and showed Erin which of the cows had freshened that morning and asked her to milk her and feed her milk to the calves. With Dan leading, Lydia milked her way down the rows of cows. There was no sign of Irv and Lydia grumbled to Dan when they paused at the end of one row.

"I bet he went off to the cattle auction. Fred will know," she said, looking around. "Normally, I'd rather he wasn't here when I'm milking 'cause he's so distracting, but I really wanted to pin him down about getting a permanent milker if Robert is going to be out of the picture for a while."

"I saw Fred go outside and Billy disappeared a few minutes ago."

"Are you worried about Billy? Today is day three," she added.

"Yeah, it is and no, Kevin is on Billy," he said, bending over the first cow in the next row.

When they straightened up from the last cow, Billy was cleaning behind the cows. The rain had stopped completely and small patches of blue sky were visible. They found Fred leaning against the barn, smoking.

"Hey, Miss Lydia. Irv said to tell you he'll call tonight. Seems he's got somebody to take Robert's place. Wish my daughter would find somebody to take Robert's place," he mumbled, shaking his head. He tossed his cigarette onto the grass and Lydia stepped on it automatically.

He was caught in a spasm of coughing and Lydia waited until he caught his breath. "Irv gone to auction, Fred?"

He nodded. "Why's he needs to be buying more cows, anyway?" Fred was already lighting up another cigarette, then dropping a lighter into his shirt pocket.

"I guess that's a yes." She shook her head at him. "It's a game with him, Fred. You should know that." She smiled at him and patted his back before she turned away and walked toward the SUV.

"I feel sorry for Fred, you know?" she said as Dan opened the door for her. She looked up at him as she sat on the seat, her legs still outside the vehicle. "His wife died five years ago of cancer and he's alone, he's lost one lung and has bad emphysema in the other, and his daughter is married to the meanest guy in town."

"Those cigarettes aren't helping," Dan said as she swung her legs inside and he closed the door.

"He told me one time that it was the only pleasure he has left. Pretty pathetic." She sighed as he climbed in the other side.

Dan didn't comment, just looked over his shoulder

at Erin. "You guys interested in Chinese take-out for dinner?"

Lydia shrugged when he looked at her. "Hey, I'm the queen of take-out. You don't have to ask me." She reached in her pocket, pulled out her cell phone, and tossed it over the seat toward Eric. "Call the Golden Wok. The number's programmed in," she said, grinning at Dan. "Frazier's, Town Pizza, and the diner are all in there too. You'd better tell Eric what you want," she added, listening to Eric's voice as he talked to Mr. Yu.

A minute later, Eric leaned forward and handed her the cell phone. "Mr. Yu said hi and wanted to know why he hasn't seen you in a while. I told him Erin was doing the cooking and he laughed." Lydia accepted the phone and stuffed it in her pocket, rolling her eyes.

"Everybody in town knows my dirty little secret," she moaned, starting the engine and then shifting into gear. "Stop smiling," she instructed Dan. "You can't cook either. And don't tell me that it's woman's work, so you're exempted, or I may have to cause you bodily harm," she threatened.

"Never." He laughed.

The kitchen was cleaned up and the twins had disappeared an hour ago, leaving Lydia sitting on the porch, a book in her lap. "I'm really too tired to even read. These four A.M. jaunts are getting old."

She looked across at Dan, sprawled in a chair with his feet up on the ottoman, his eyes closed. She laughed softly when he didn't respond. His face was relaxed and she could see his chest rising rhythmically as he slept. It was a shame to wake him but he would be more comfortable sleeping in the bed at the cottage than contorted in a chair here.

He woke the instant she touched his arm, his eyes wide open and alert, his body tensed. "Sorry, I fell asleep," he muttered, pulling himself up in the chair.

"Yeah. You need to go to bed. Come on," she said, pulling on his arm.

Instead of letting her pull him upright, he pulled back, and she landed neatly in his lap. Both arms came around her, holding her tight against his chest. She settled there, looking at his face so close to hers, and then she leaned the few inches closer and kissed him. As kisses went, Lydia thought, it was pretty tentative, but he didn't let it stay that way. He welcomed her mouth, slanting his head for better contact. His tongue touched her bottom lip and, suddenly, her whole body felt as hot as his mouth. One arm was around her back and his fingers rubbed up and down her side, making her shiver, even as the kiss continued. She managed to free one arm and slip her hand over his shoulder until her fingers were playing in the hair at the nape of his neck. His fingers stilled as he pulled back slightly and then let his lips move along her jaw. When he came back to her mouth, he left a light kiss at each corner. Lydia sighed against his mouth.

"I think I like this a lot," she admitted, rubbing her

forehead against his jaw, then smiling when he angled his head and kissed her ear.

"Did I mention that I've started to really like the smell of cows?" he whispered into her ear.

"That's so romantic," she said as she pressed a kiss to his jaw. Her lips moved against his skin as she murmured, "I like it too, particularly on you."

"Are you saying that I stink?" he said, letting his breath tickle her ear.

"Well, a shower might be a good idea," she said, teasing his lips with her own, "especially if you're going to be hanging out close to the bad guys tonight."

His hand resumed its slide up and down her side while his other hand rested on her hip, pulling her closer. Lydia forgot about any other sense but touch as his hand moved from her hip to her stomach and rested there while his other hand continued to stroke her side. His mouth was moving over hers, exploring, teasing, consuming.

When he pulled back, it was just far enough to look in her eyes. She sighed against his lips and he held her, cradling her against his chest, until she raised her head. "You are really good at this seduction stuff."

"I hope so, but only with you, Lydia."

She sighed as she got to her feet. "Only with you, Dan," she admitted, admiring his dimple as he smiled at her. She leaned over and kissed that dimple, then stepped away when he pulled himself up from the chair.

"Okay, I guess I'll take a shower before I go sit in a

tree for half the night. I'd rather sit in a chair with you for the whole night, but duty dictates otherwise." His gaze was on her mouth and he reached for her, bringing her against his chest. He kissed her gently and she pulled closer, her kiss more insistent. " 'Night, Dan."

"You're pretty good at seduction yourself." He grinned, opening the screen door and stepping out onto the porch. Lydia followed him out and watched as he walked down the path, turning around once to smile at her before it was too dark to see him any longer.

She stood out on the porch until the persistent buzzing of a mosquito sent her inside. She automatically locked up, turning off the lights as she went through the house. She *did* need a shower. She could smell the faint essence of cow on her skin and it reminded her of the smell of Dan's skin as she sat cradled in his arms, her nose against his neck.

The shower felt good and she fell into bed ten minutes later, determined to stop thinking about being that close to a man's skin, that aware of his smell, not just of cow but his soap, his shampoo, his sweat. Boy, she had it bad, she thought, just before she fell asleep.

Chapter Eighteen

It had been another long watch. The shadows were familiar and unchanging. Even the coyotes avoided the area this night. Dan shifted slightly at a sign of movement in the trees beyond the shack.

The white bandage covering his nose was easily visible even before Billy was completely out of the trees and walking toward the shack. The night-vision goggles showed Dan the tattered shirt, torn jeans, and scruffy beard that Billy wore like a uniform. A couple days in the hospital had probably helped with the smell and his skin and hair had gotten some attention. They probably used a fire hose, Dan thought cynically. If he had been a nurse at the hospital when they had dropped Billy off, he wouldn't have touched the guy without a mask and gloves. And he would have added earplugs to block the whining.

"What's he up to?" Dan wondered as he watched Billy look around. Instead of going inside as usual, he hunkered down with his back to the shack wall. After a few minutes, Dan shook his head and cursed silently. The fool was waiting for the pickup. He must have decided to try to make a better deal for himself, or he was set on informing, in hopes of gaining favor. So much for trusting this jerk.

Dan lowered himself from the platform, keeping his body in the shelter of the trunk of the tree before dropping to the ground. He punched Kevin's number into his cell phone and when Kevin picked up after one ring, spoke into the mouthpiece. The early-morning birdcall covered the almost inaudible words and he pocketed the phone a few seconds later as he started to work his way in a wide circle, aiming for the back of the shack. Billy was still crouched against the building's front wall, and Dan could see him picking and biting his nails, totally involved in the mindless activity.

Dan needed to get Billy out of sight before the pickup car arrived and he needed to get the package away from Billy and stowed in the shed. The eastern sky was lightening and he didn't have much time. Billy looked up as Dan stepped around the corner of the building, then stumbled to his feet, his eyes wild, pulling a knife from his waistband. He waved it around, words spewing from his mouth. Dan figured about every other one was some form of filth. Dan had his Glock drawn but Billy took a step toward him, obviously terrified and then rushed forward. Billy had the look of a man desperate enough to kill. Dan dodged the raised knife and before he could bring the gun down on the side of Billy's head, there was a thud and the man pitched forward onto his face without a sound. Dan leaped for the cover of the building and looked out to see a figure emerge from the trees fifteen feet away.

Lydia stopped next to Billy's inert figure and grinned.

"What are you doing here?" Dan exploded, although it came out in a hiss as he sucked in his breath and tried to keep from shouting. He grabbed her arm and pulled her behind the building, out of sight of the track through the woods.

"I was an excellent pitcher in high school," she said, turning to look down at Billy who was starting to moan. "I saw him head this way as I was leaving Irv's. I would have stayed out of sight, except he tried to kill you," she said, turning back to Dan and pounding his chest with her fist.

"Okay, okay," he whispered, grabbing her hand. "I'll thank you later. I've got to get him out of sight. The pickup car will be here any minute. I think he was about to try a little double-cross on us," he said, bending over Billy and searching his pockets. He found the package in his jeans pocket and stepped in the door of the shed. He was back in a few seconds, without the package, pulling a length of nylon cord from his vest pocket. He yanked Billy's arms behind his back, tied them, and then secured his feet before dragging him behind the shed and back into the trees. Lydia followed, picking up Billy's feet and boosting him along while Dan dragged him by the shoulders.

A loud moan came from Billy when Dan dropped him prone on the ground again. "I need to gag this sucker before he gives us away," he muttered and saw Lydia sit on the ground and quickly pull off her sneaker and sock. She handed the sock to Dan and slid her foot back into her sneaker. Dan bent to shove the sock in Billy's mouth as she quickly removed the lace from her sneaker and handed it to him to secure the gag in place.

The birdcall had stopped and Dan was suddenly aware of the faint sound of a car engine. He grabbed Lydia and pushed her down behind the wide trunk of an oak. Her white T-shirt was like a beacon in the faint light and he pushed her down flat, coming down on top of her, covering her with his own black-clad body. She didn't make a sound, just turned her head to the side so she could breathe. The engine noise came closer and they could hear a car door opening and the faint sound of footsteps in the duff and leaf mold underfoot.

Dan looked up, slitting his eyes, and watched as the guy he had seen at Frazier's, wearing the same sport jacket, walked back to the black SUV, got in, and closed the door. The engine noise gradually moved away and Dan waited another couple of minutes before lifting his head again. He kissed Lydia's ear before rolling off her and getting to his feet. He reached a hand down to her and lifted her to her feet. With his arms around her, he said, "Don't do that again. You almost gave me a heart attack, Lydia," he growled, shaking her slightly, then tightening his arms around her again.

Lydia stood quietly, holding on to him, glad he was safe, glad she was safe. She looked over at Billy, trussed up and gagged thirty feet away, hidden behind another tree and didn't feel a single pang of sympathy for him, or any real concern for his fate. "You do this kind of stuff all the time?" she asked, turning her head back to Dan.

"Nah. Most of the time, it's pretty dull." He grinned. The sky had brightened enough so he could see her face clearly and recognized the disbelief in her eyes. "Billy was going to talk to those guys and we don't need him blowing this whole operation. Now, come on," he said, loosening his hold on her and turning toward Billy. "Our friend here is going to wake up any minute and I don't want him to see you."

He bent over to pick up Billy's knife with his gloved hand and dropped it into a plastic bag he took from his vest pocket before dropping the bag and its contents onto Billy's back. "Let's go," he said to Lydia, tugging on her arm.

"Do we just leave him here?"

"Yeah. Kevin is on his way and he'll have a sheriff's deputy with him." Dan was hauling her through the trees, circling back to the tree stand. He needed to get Lydia out of the area. Billy's whole family lived in this town and they definitely didn't need to know that Lydia was involved in this, and Billy would be sure to tell them if he recognized her.

Billy was a very small piece of this whole operation but he'd had the potential for breaking it apart. The guys involved in this neighborhood would have been quick to pass on a warning to everyone in the line of suppliers and distributors and they would have all disappeared by the time the agency was ready to move in on them. Dan didn't think the agency's work had been compromised by this little episode, but he'd be glad when the whole thing was wrapped up. Billy would be put away, out of sight, until it was over, and probably for a long stretch to come, after this morning's adventure.

While Lydia waited at the base of the tree, Dan scrambled up to the platform and retrieved his pack. When he dropped to the ground again, the pack was slung over his shoulder and he grinned at Lydia, reaching for her and holding her tight for a minute. "Where's your truck?"

"I left it on the old access road to the airport," she answered, nodding her head to the northeast. "There used to be a firing range on this side of the airport property and the road into it is still mostly open. I drove in there far enough so the truck couldn't be seen from the road. Billy's car is pulled off on the main road, in plain sight. I wonder what he was thinking?" she said, shaking her head. "Those guys in the SUV will have seen it."

"Not thinking seems to be Billy's modus operandi," Dan replied, taking her hand and starting to jog in the direction she had indicated. They followed a deer trail that wound through the trees, heading generally northeast. Lydia pulled him to a stop after a quarter mile and pointed farther east. They changed direction and five minutes later emerged onto an overgrown dirt road. The sun was above the horizon now and glinted off metal a hundred yards to their left.

Dan tossed his pack on the front seat of Lydia's SUV and then walked around to lean in the window next to her. "Go home and stay there, Lydia."

"You're welcome, Dan."

"I know." He sighed. "You want me to thank you for throwing a rock. But," he added, "you put yourself in danger, Lydia. Go home now before I start yelling at you."

Lydia leaned over, kissed him on the lips, and then reached to start the engine. "Save your voice. I'm not going to be impressed. I'd do it again in a heartbeat."

Dan just looked at her for a minute, then pulled his head out of the window, a smile crinkling his eyes, his dimple showing as his lips turned up. "I'm still going to yell at you and then I'm going to kiss you 'til you get weak in the knees and promise me anything."

"Anytime, Dan, anytime," she retorted, matching his smile before she put the vehicle in gear and backed slowly away toward the blacktop.

Dan headed back to the shack, jogging as fast as he dared. The sun barely penetrated the trees and once he found the deer trail, it was an easy run. A sheriff's patrol car was standing close to the shack and Kevin and a uniformed deputy were loading Billy into the backseat when he stopped next to it. Billy's face was covered with fresh dirt and his nose, under the bandage, looked crooked. His whiney voice reached Dan, complaining that he had been attacked and his nose broken again.

The deputy caught sight of him and crouched, drawing his gun. Dan stopped, recognizing Butch Fraleigh. He was still working as a deputy, he realized. Kevin said something in a low voice and the deputy holstered his gun. "Hey, I thought you made detective, Butch," Dan said, walking forward.

"Yeah, I did. Starts next week. I got assigned to this duty 'til then." He looked at Dan suspiciously. "Why didn't you tell me you were part of this op?"

Dan raised his eyebrows. "Would *you* have told me?" he asked.

Butch shrugged and didn't answer, turning away to the front of the car.

Kevin raised his eyebrows and Dan gestured for him to move farther away from the car. "What's with him?" Kevin indicated the deputy now sitting in the driver's seat.

"I met him a week or so ago. I declined to inform him of my real business here. He's not pleased, I guess." He grinned at Kevin, adding, "He's an old friend of Lydia's."

"Seems like a jerk to me," Kevin commented.

Dan laughed, glancing back over his shoulder. "You always could call 'em, Kev."

With his back to Billy, Dan filled Kevin in, explaining the lump on the back of Billy's head. "It would be better if I just said that the lump was from where I hit him when he came at me with the knife, rather than explain that Lydia threw a rock and beaned him. His face did hit the ground when he fell and he never saw her 'cause she knocked him out cold." He looked at Kevin, who shook his head.

"I didn't see anybody else out here, Dan. You can tell me all about it later, after I get rid of Billy and the deputy over there." He jerked his head back toward the car. "I'll be in touch," he said, turning back to the car and climbing in the passenger seat.

It had been a long night and Dan was tired and hungry. He was also ticked off at Lydia for putting herself in danger, although he had to admit to himself that the thought of her defending him from an assault made his blood heat up even more than it did just thinking about her. But he had to make her understand that she needed to stay apart from all this. The people they were dealing with wouldn't hesitate to hurt or kill her if they thought she was a threat.

He picked up his pace as he jogged toward the cottage. He needed food and sleep before he tackled her. She would look at him and smile and deny she was in danger. She would argue that she knew this area and the people and she wasn't so naive that she'd risk her life. And Billy would never hurt her. He had known her since she was a child. And he would have to tell her that Billy would hurt his own mother if he thought he was threatened by her. People like Billy had no morals, no ethics, no remorse. They had one goal—self-preservation.

He wanted to see her but reasoned that she was probably sleeping. While he had been perched up in his tree, she had been milking cows . . . and noticing Billy's movements. She was a scientist, a trained observer. Naturally, she would have noticed any deviation in Billy's pattern.

He wasn't surprised that he found her sleeping on the swing on his front porch when he walked up the steps. She was curled on her side, her legs drawn up, barely fitting the swing. Her head was resting on one arm, her other hand dangling off the edge of the seat.

Squatting next to her, he bent forward enough to let his breath touch her lips and he smiled when she sighed in her sleep. He blew lightly on her face until she opened her eyes and then he kissed her gently. She smiled against his mouth and lifted her arm around his shoulder and held him for a minute.

When she moved to sit up, Dan stood, looking down at her.

"No yelling, Dan. You're right about Billy and you're right about the danger and I'm not trained for this." She paused and looked into his eyes. "I'm glad you're home safe."

He pulled her to her feet and against his chest, holding her tightly for a minute. Then he pushed her away a few inches and smiled. "Your pitching arm is very impressive."

"League champions three years running," she bragged. She hesitated before asking, "Will you come for breakfast?"

He let his hands slide down her back before letting his arms fall to his side and stepping back a pace. "The report will take a while and then I need to sleep. I'll find you later," he promised as she turned toward the steps. When she jumped from the top step to the ground, he laughed and she waved as she jogged down the driveway. Flirt appeared at her side and she looked down at her and touched the top of the dog's head. He could see her talking to the dog as they moved farther away. He had noticed that she spoke to that dog as if they were best friends. She was probably telling her about her morning adventure, and the dog would listen to every word.

His pack was sitting in front of the door and he scooped it up and went inside. After he showered and dressed in clean shorts and a T-shirt, he went to the desk and started to write his report. He was skilled with words and he wrote a report that was concise and factual without embellishments. Assistance from a civilian was not mentioned.

By the time he was done, his shoulders were aching and he stretched once to relieve the tension. He sent the report to his boss by e-mail and shut down the computer. He needed to get serious about finishing the rewrite of his latest novel but that wasn't going to happen this morning. This morning he was going to get a few hours' sleep and then he was going to find Lydia and help her with whatever she was doing. He was going to live a normal life for the rest of the day, if he could.

He went out onto the porch and looked out over the farm. The fields were green; the pond water reflected the sunlight. The old apple trees marched in rows over the hill and the air was still. There was no sight or sound of traffic. He heard a sheep cough in the distance and that was the only sound to break the silence of the morning.

He had some idea of the work that went into maintaining the order he saw all around. Buildings had to be painted and repaired; fences had to be built and rebuilt; fields had to be mowed and plowed and planted. Crops had to be harvested and stored; animals required care and attention every day.

Lydia had told him that over eighty percent of the working farms in this state required an outside income to keep them afloat. Somebody had to work off the farm to bring in enough cash to pay the bills because the farm couldn't generate enough income to be self-sufficient. He wondered if that was true all over the country.

People like Lydia worked to make this life viable. They studied and researched and thought of innovative ways to market what they could grow in their particular soil and their particular climate. Maybe there was hope for these small farms. Maybe the millions who bleated about the need for open space would continue to have it if these farms survived.

And maybe he was thinking that he could stay here . . . with Lydia. He stood there motionless for a minute, rewinding and then replaying that last thought, no longer seeing the fields or the orchard. A house with a big porch and little kids playing in the yard and a wife who studied and worked and played and wore her hair in a ponytail and defended him and loved him created a pretty pleasant image. It made him smile and shake his head. Putting a name to the woman in the image was a no-brainer. He could only hope she had the same future in mind.

He looked toward the barns when the rumble of a four-wheeler sounded from that direction. He saw Eric drive out of the machinery shed and start down the lane, and knew that he was going to check on the sheep and cows. With his brain and body starting to protest the long night, he went into the cottage and turned the fan on before he stretched out on top of the bed.

Chapter Nineteen

Lydia was grinning. That nobody was there to see her didn't stop the grin from spreading, as she continued to enter numbers into the computer. After a morning of trimming and cleaning garlic, measuring and weighing the bulbs, the figures in front of her made her want to jump up and shout. There was still more to do and more numbers to gather but her theory had just received a tremendous boost.

If the research being done over the last two years on the breakdown products of wool and their effect on soil nutrients proved what the researchers suspected, using wool for mulch would get some very good press. Adding nutrients to the soil with the same material that controlled soil temperature and moisture would make it an unbeatable product. Add to that the fact that it broke down naturally, didn't need to be landfilled, and didn't harm the environment or use up petroleum reserves, and the whole sheep industry may have found a way to survive and prosper.

She knew better than to get completely carried away before she had all the information, but she couldn't help being excited. She needed to tell somebody, okay, brag to somebody *now*. She could tell Dan. It had only taken a couple of weeks for Dan to become so important to her that she wanted to share everything with him. She reminded herself that he was only here on an assignment that would be over in a few days. And then he would leave and she would finish her dissertation and defend it and then what?

Well, she wanted more than that. She wanted a man who loved her first and always, a house in the country, kids to spoil and nurture, another research project. That wasn't so much, after all. She already knew where to find the man, glancing toward the cottage as she walked back to the house. That morning, when she had followed Billy and had seen him attacking Dan, she had reacted instinctively to protect him, even though her intellect told her that he was more than capable of protecting himself. When she had dropped Billy with a pitch that her coach would have been proud of, she knew, right then, that Dan Madison had become more important than her own safety, than her own life.

Was she in love with him? It sure felt like it to her.

She could see Erin through the kitchen window as she came up the back steps and when she stepped into the kitchen, she saw Dan leaning against the counter. When he looked up and saw her, a smile of such pleasure crossed his face that she stopped in midstride. He kept looking at her and smiling until Erin poked him in the ribs and pushed a plate full of sandwiches into his hands.

Erin looked around and grinned. "Right on time, Lydia. Meatloaf sandwiches, chips, and pickles for lunch. Go clean up," she said, pointing to the dirt clinging to Lydia's hands.

"I will," Lydia replied, walking toward the door to the dining room before she stopped and turned around to watch Dan carry the plate of sandwiches toward the porch. He looked at her and winked as he passed, and she couldn't stop the smile that spread across her own face.

She had it so-o-o-o bad, she thought as she scrubbed her hands and then splashed water on her face. She hoped that the cold water would cool her down enough to pass Erin's scrutiny. She certainly wasn't ready to broadcast her infatuation to her fourteen-year-old niece. Not that she stood a chance, she realized, from the look Erin gave her as she came onto the porch. Dan held a chair for her next to his and Erin positively smirked at her across the table. No doubt she thought she had either engineered a romance herself, or at the least was privy to it from the start.

"So, how did you manage enough meatloaf for sandwiches in a half hour?" Lydia asked, looking at Erin, hoping to distract her from noticing that Dan had put his arm on the back of her chair and they were sitting way too close together.

Erin grinned at Dan and then turned her attention to Lydia. "Microwave," she said, taking a huge bite from her sandwich.

Fortunately for Lydia, Eric wanted to know if they were going to work on the garlic after lunch. "No. I think I'll just clean enough to take to the farmers' market. It's pretty fresh but Faith called from the market to tell me that people are already asking for it. Why don't you guys take the afternoon off," she suggested. "If you want to go to town, I can drop you off on the way to the market and pick you up after the milking is done."

"Okay. You up for a movie, Erin?" Eric asked, reaching across her to snag another half of a sandwich. "We can make the afternoon matinee if you want."

Erin looked at Lydia. "Don't you need us for the milking?"

"Not anymore." Lydia grinned. "Irv called this morning while you were still in bed to tell me he had found somebody. Pete Hudson called him, looking for work."

She looked at Dan and explained. "Pete was a herdsman for a dairy farther upstate 'til the owner sold out. I remember him from when he worked over at Kilmer's years ago. My Dad always liked him. Said he was really good with the cows. If I remember correctly, he also said that Irving ought to hire him on to take over the dairy and run the farm so he'd have one good man instead of two or three losers."

"That may happen now," Dan remarked, turning his head to look at Lydia directly.

"Yes, it may," Lydia agreed.

"Hey, what do you guys know that we don't?" Erin complained, looking from Lydia to Dan and back again.

"Lots of stuff," Lydia said, getting up from her chair. "You okay with steak on the grill for dinner? I think I forgot to tell you that Dan's friend Kevin, and Sophie are coming for dinner," she said to Erin.

"Neat. Can you get some tomatoes from the market while you're there? Ours aren't ripe yet. I can make some potato salad. Do you think Faith has any sweet corn yet?" she asked, gathering plates to take to the kitchen. "What kind of pie do you like, Dan?" directing her attention toward him.

"Um, lemon meringue," he admitted, smiling at her.

"Excellent. I make the best meringue you'll ever taste," she said over her shoulder. "When do you want us to be ready to go, Lydia?" she asked, lowering the pile of dishes into the sink.

"A half hour okay with you?" Lydia turned to ask Eric as he followed her into the kitchen, carrying glasses in both hands.

"You bet. Thanks, Lydia."

"Why don't you go get the garlic ready while I wash

these dishes?" Erin asked, running water into the sink. "Can you drop me at the bookstore? I can walk down to the theater when I'm done," she said, rapidly loading the dishwasher. When Dan moved next to her to help, she shook her head at him and tilted her head toward Lydia, who was already walking down the porch steps. "Maybe you could help Lydia," she said, grinning at him.

Dan caught up with Lydia before she had gone a hundred feet and he reached for her fingers.

She blinked when he asked, "So who's Faith?"

"She and her husband, Hugh, own Hamilton Orchards and the farmers' market where Dad sells his garlic. Faith grew up here and was a couple of years ahead of me in school," she went on. "She met Hugh while she was studying agricultural economics at Penn State and he was studying pomology." She glanced at him and saw the puzzled look on his face. "The science of fruit production," she explained. "Apple, peach, berries, mostly. After they married, they moved back here to take over the orchards when her father decided to retire. They grow apples and peaches, red and black raspberries." She looked at him questioningly. "Why do you want to know about Faith? I'd swear that neither she nor Hugh are involved in the drug business," she stated emphatically.

He pulled her to a stop and looked at her. "I never thought so, Lydia. I just want to know your friends."

"Why?"

He slid his arms around her, looking at her with

such a serious expression on his face that her breathing stopped for a second. "Because your friends are part of you and I want to know you."

"Oh." She looked into his eyes, then at his mouth, and finally dropped her eyes to his chest. He continued to hold her until she stepped away and started walking down the path again, catching his hand in hers as she moved away.

She slid her fingers away from his as she pulled open the screen door of the drying barn. The whir of the fans ventilating the inside of the building dominated the atmosphere. It was relatively cool inside and the bundles of plants hanging from the poles looked eerie in the dimness.

Lydia released the string holding several bundles aloft and carried the plants to a table set up near the row of windows. Dan watched while she cut the bulbs from the plants with heavy scissors, leaving an inch or two of stalk, and then flipped the bulb around and trimmed the root mass. He reached for another pair of scissors and started trimming the next bulb.

Other than the hum of the fans and the snip and crunch of the scissors, they worked in a comfortable silence. Within minutes, there were dozens of garlic bulbs, separated from their stalks and leaves and with the root masses trimmed, lying on the table.

"Now comes the tedious part," Lydia said, sitting down and indicating the chair next to her. "You ready for this, Dan?"

He just grinned at her as he sat next to her. Her fingers were practiced as she used a toothbrush to clean any remaining dirt from the trimmed roots and then turned the bulb upright. Her thumb nail scored the outer layer and she quickly peeled it away, leaving a shiny, clean, off-white bulb. With the brush, she quickly removed the few traces of dirt at the base of the bulb and then held it up for inspection.

"The customer doesn't want to know that this bulb ever touched dirt, so cleaning is critical. That outer layer I removed is a bulb wrapper, one of several that protect the cloves." She shrugged. "Sometimes you can get them clean enough by just brushing the outside of the bulb, but this is heavy, clay soil and it tends to cling, so it's frequently easier and quicker to just take the outer layer right off." The whole time she was explaining the procedure, she was cleaning another bulb.

Dan's fingers felt clumsy when he started but he quickly acquired the knack of peeling the outer bulb wrapper, taking ninety percent of the dirt with it. "With the amount of garlic you grow, this must take a lot of hours. It doesn't require an advanced degree in astrophysics to do this, but how do you keep the help from rebelling?"

"Believe me," she said, laughing, "it's more like a party down here usually. A neighbor's grandson visits them for a few weeks every summer and he's always ready to work. He's the same age as the twins. There's a local high school girl who's helped out here since she was twelve. The music is loud and all I have to do is provide food and drink to keep them working."

Fifteen minutes later, while Dan cleaned the last bulb, Lydia stood and grabbed a bag from the shelf behind her and began placing the bulbs inside. "Garlic will bruise, just like an apple, if it gets banged around. Then it won't keep. This hard neck garlic doesn't keep as long as the soft neck varieties but it will keep 'til Christmas if you treat it right," she said, carefully lifting the bag and carrying it to a scale. She scribbled the weight on a piece of paper and shoved it into the bag and then wrote the date and weight in a notebook next to the scale on the table.

Dan took the bag from her as they left the barn, letting the screen door slap closed behind him. It was much hotter outside than in the barn and Lydia grinned at him. "Dad built this building right here because it stays shaded a good part of the day. Drying garlic can be tricky. It requires a fairly constant temperature, not above eighty degrees or so, or it starts to cook. And with all the moisture in the stalks and leaves, good ventilation is absolutely necessary."

The twins were sitting on the porch when they climbed the steps and Eric took the bag of garlic from Dan. "We have to clean up a little," Lydia said to him as she passed. "Be right out."

They dropped the twins at the bookstore and then Lydia drove a couple of miles on the main road before turning into the parking area next to a farmers' stand.

She grabbed the bag of garlic out of the backseat and carried it toward the building. There were plots of herbs growing out front and flowers lined the fence that separated the farmers' market from the road. There was a small permanent building made larger in three directions by green striped canvas awnings stretched over an aluminum framework. Shelves and bins lined the walls and the perimeter of the covered area. Jars of jams and jellies took up one whole shelf and Lydia pointed them out to Dan as they passed. "Faith makes all that in her spare time," she told him.

A young woman with short, curly brown hair walked around the corner of the building, carrying a basket filled with potatoes. Dan went to take it from her and she released it to him with a smile. "Hey, Lydia. Who's your handsome, chivalrous friend here?"

Dan grinned at her and followed her with the basket. Lydia made the introductions while he set the basket in place on a table, and then turned. Faith was eyeing him up and down and his grin got wider. "Nice legs, Lydia. Great shoulders too. You run and lift weights, right?" she said, winking at him. He laughed and admitted to both.

"Stop that, Faith! You're a married woman," Lydia chided.

"Just commenting on the scenery," Faith said, grinning again. "You want to try some of this jam I made last night? The raspberries were spectacular this year. I was kind of worried that they'd mold too fast

---

ee.

vil-
ing as-
ether, she

gether every

ashed green and
grocery store lot
ring. "No, you're not

efore releasing his hand
the time Lydia had hers
front and pulling her door
stand up, he leaned over and

find us some steaks," he invited,
ss the lot toward the entrance. "Yo
am cone and a nap before it's time to

u ordering me around, Agent Madi
gged a cart with her free hand as he
the door. Then he smiled at her, slid

because of all the rain, so I've been makir
batches of jam to use them up." She hande
cracker covered with bright red jam and watc
he bit it in half and licked his lips.

When he rolled his eyes in appreci
grabbed a jar off the shelf and handed it t
one who appreciates my jam gets a free
explained, turning to look at Lydia, wh
paper bag with tomatoes. "Did you br
Lydia?"

"In the bag on the counter. Are
toes, Faith?"

"I wish. No, ours aren't ripe
maybe." She paused while she
next to Lydia. "They're from a
She looked over her shoulder a
bag with sweet corn. "So, tell r

"Yes."

"Just 'yes'? No details? (

"Nope." Lydia moved ov
and started filling a bag. "
potato salad," she remarkeu, a
for more information.

"Guess it's serious if you won't tell me anyu..g
think I'll go over and ask him."

"You do and you're dead meat, Faith," Lydia
growled. "If I promise to reveal all as soon as I know
it myself, will you leave him alone?"

"Hey, I thought she was pretty quick on the uptake.
She didn't embarrass me, if that's what you're worried
about," he said, reaching out to lay his hand on her knee.

"What did she say to you to get you all bothered?"

"Nothing, really," she said, concentrating on th
traffic and not on his hand, still resting on her kn
She stopped at the traffic light in the center of th
lage and looked over at him. "She was just mak
sumptions out of nothing. Because we're tog

"I thought we were closer to being to
day. Am I wrong?" he asked quietly.

Lydia turned left when the light f
waited until she had pulled into th
and parked the car before answe
wrong," she admitted.

He squeezed her knee b
and opening his door. B
open, he was around th
wide. Before she cou
kissed her.

"Come on. Let
pulling her acro
need an ice cre
milking."

"Are yo
She sna
her to

around her waist, and hustled her down the aisle toward the meat cases.

The answering machine light was blinking when they walked into the kitchen. Lydia punched the button to play the message and listened to her mother's voice as she dumped the potatoes into a big pot and ran water over them. With her free hand, she grabbed a glass baking dish and asked Dan to open the package of meat and lay the meat in the dish. With the potatoes on the stove and a timer set, she found a bottle of barbecue sauce in the refrigerator and poured it over the meat and then covered it with plastic wrap. Her mother's voice penetrated her absorption with the food and she realized that her mother had called to tell them that they would be home for supper the next night.

"I bet Dad is worrying about his garlic," she remarked to Dan as she erased the message. "He's probably been hurrying Mom across the country, trying to get home." She looked up from the dish she was carrying to grin at Dan. "Mom likes to stop at every bend in the road to check out the local attractions."

The meat went into the refrigerator to marinate and she sighed, suddenly feeling her early-morning work and lack of sleep. Dan wrapped his arms around her and let one hand slide up and down her back. "Why don't you go take a power nap? I'll mind the potatoes."

Lydia objected but very faintly, enjoying the

sensation of Dan's hand rubbing her back and she sighed again as she leaned against him. "I could go to sleep right here," she admitted. Her face was nestled against his neck when she asked, "Did you sleep this morning?"

"Several hours," he answered. "It's your turn now. I'll go get my laptop and work out on the porch. I know how to check the potatoes and how to drain them. Go now," he said, turning her in his arms and then giving her a little push toward the hallway. "I'll call you when it's time to get up."

Dan jogged back to the cottage to collect his laptop. When he got back, water was splashing onto the stove from the boiling potatoes and he went inside to turn the heat down under the pot.

He was surprised when the timer went off. The rewrite was almost done and he was happy with it, he thought, saving the file before going into the kitchen. He poked the potatoes with a fork and decided they were done, then lifted the pot to the sink and poured off the water. He peered into the pot, keeping away from the steam rising from the sink. Some of the skins had opened and he supposed that was a good sign as far as doneness was concerned. Or maybe not.

He left the pot to cool in the sink and went back to his laptop. He could let Lydia sleep for another forty-five minutes before they needed to get to Irv's.

She grabbed the bag of garlic out of the backseat and carried it toward the building. There were plots of herbs growing out front and flowers lined the fence that separated the farmers' market from the road. There was a small permanent building made larger in three directions by green striped canvas awnings stretched over an aluminum framework. Shelves and bins lined the walls and the perimeter of the covered area. Jars of jams and jellies took up one whole shelf and Lydia pointed them out to Dan as they passed. "Faith makes all that in her spare time," she told him.

A young woman with short, curly brown hair walked around the corner of the building, carrying a basket filled with potatoes. Dan went to take it from her and she released it to him with a smile. "Hey, Lydia. Who's your handsome, chivalrous friend here?"

Dan grinned at her and followed her with the basket. Lydia made the introductions while he set the basket in place on a table, and then turned. Faith was eyeing him up and down and his grin got wider. "Nice legs, Lydia. Great shoulders too. You run and lift weights, right?" she said, winking at him. He laughed and admitted to both.

"Stop that, Faith! You're a married woman," Lydia chided.

"Just commenting on the scenery," Faith said, grinning again. "You want to try some of this jam I made last night? The raspberries were spectacular this year. I was kind of worried that they'd mold too fast because of all the rain, so I've been making huge batches of jam to use them up." She handed Dan a cracker covered with bright red jam and watched while he bit it in half and licked his lips.

When he rolled his eyes in appreciation, Faith grabbed a jar off the shelf and handed it to him. "Anyone who appreciates my jam gets a free sample," she explained, turning to look at Lydia, who was filling a paper bag with tomatoes. "Did you bring some garlic, Lydia?"

"In the bag on the counter. Are these your tomatoes, Faith?"

"I wish. No, ours aren't ripe yet. Another week maybe." She paused while she walked over to stand next to Lydia. "They're from a farm in New Jersey." She looked over her shoulder at Dan, who was filling a bag with sweet corn. "So, tell me, Lydia. Is he special?"

"Yes."

"Just 'yes'? No details? Come on," she coaxed.

"Nope." Lydia moved over to the basket of potatoes and started filling a bag. "These Kennebecs make great potato salad," she remarked, ignoring Faith's demand for more information.

"Guess it's serious if you won't tell me anything. I think I'll go over and ask him."

"You do and you're dead meat, Faith," Lydia growled. "If I promise to reveal all as soon as I know it myself, will you leave him alone?"

"Maybe," Faith said over her shoulder as she moved toward the register to check out another customer.

Lydia lined up her bags of tomatoes and potatoes on the counter and then went over to take the bag of sweet corn dangling from Dan's fingers.

Lydia fished in her purse for money but Dan slid a twenty onto the counter before her hand came out of the purse. "I'm buying, Lydia. You feed me all the time, so no argument."

"Dang. I was going to make you buy the steaks."

"I'll do that too." He smiled at Faith who had been listening to the exchange.

"She feeds you, does she?" Faith looked back and forth from Dan to Lydia and then to Dan again, grinning as she handed him the change.

Lydia rolled her eyes at her before she grabbed the bags off the counter. Dan reached around to take them from her and Faith grinned at him again. "See you guys," she called as they moved away.

"I have to stop at the grocery store for the steaks and then I'm going to get the biggest soft ice cream cone they make. I deserve it for putting up with Faith," she declared, opening the back of the SUV so Dan could the bags inside. After she had climbed in the driver seat, she continued, "We've been friends for I'm she's been trying to matchmake all that time. out of she added, glancing at Dan as she pulled king lot.

"Hey, I thought she was pretty quick on the uptake. She didn't embarrass me, if that's what you're worried about," he said, reaching out to lay his hand on her knee. "What did she say to you to get you all bothered?"

"Nothing, really," she said, concentrating on the traffic and not on his hand, still resting on her knee. She stopped at the traffic light in the center of the village and looked over at him. "She was just making assumptions out of nothing. Because we're together, she assumed we're *together*."

"I thought we were closer to being together every day. Am I wrong?" he asked quietly.

Lydia turned left when the light flashed green and waited until she had pulled into the grocery store lot and parked the car before answering. "No, you're not wrong," she admitted.

He squeezed her knee before releasing his hand and opening his door. By the time Lydia had hers open, he was around the front and pulling her door wide. Before she could stand up, he leaned over and kissed her.

"Come on. Let's find us some steaks," he invited, pulling her across the lot toward the entrance. "You need an ice cream cone and a nap before it's time to milking."

"Are you ordering me around, Agent Madi? She snagged a cart with her free hand as he m her to the door. Then he smiled at her, slid

Chapter Twenty

He smelled her toothpaste before he felt her hand rest on his shoulder. She must have brushed her teeth when she got up, he thought, reaching his hand up to hold hers in place on his shoulder. He tugged gently on her hand until she leaned over his shoulder and he turned his head and kissed her. Her breath was flavored with mint and he brushed his lips back and forth over hers. "Mmm, you taste good."

She stayed leaning over his shoulder even after he moved his head and she looked at him, studying his face for a minute, before she landed a quick kiss on his cheek, aiming for that dimple, and stood up, put her arms around his shoulders from behind and held him.

He barely had the presence of mind to save his file before she lifted her arms away. "I guess you feel better." He laughed, closing the laptop and turning to look at her. She had sheet creases on one side of her face and was smothering a yawn.

"Yes, definitely." She nodded. "Are you ready to go do this? You don't have to."

Before she could continue, he got up and pulled her against his chest. "I want to help you, Lydia, whatever you're doing. Now let's go," he said, steering her toward the door.

The cows were in their stanchions, the milking machine motors were humming, the cows were eating and the man moving from cow to cow was well on his way down the first row of cows. Fred was leaning against the wall, grinning, when Lydia stepped inside.

"You look pretty happy, Fred," she said above the noise of motors.

"Miss Lydia, that new man is a marvel. And he's polite to me too," he said, as if that was such a novel happening. He was amazed. "Treats the cows real good," he said, nodding his head.

Lydia moved off toward the "marvel," leaving Dan to talk to Fred. Pete Hudson was fiftyish, balding, and talking to the cows as Lydia approached. His voice was low and soothing, and he touched each cow gently and calmly. Irv had really lucked out, Lydia thought, waiting for Pete to notice her. When he straightened up, Lydia smiled, offering her hand.

He nodded at her. "I remember you from when you

were a little kid, following your daddy around. I think I was working over at Kilmer's then," he mused. "Your daddy still raising beef?"

"Sure." She grinned. "And some sheep now," she added.

"Pesky critters, I always thought," he admitted, looking over her shoulder. Dan was walking toward them and Lydia introduced him. She immediately saw the speculation in Pete's eyes and groaned. "What is it with everybody?" she grumbled, moving away to let Pete keep working. She felt Dan's hand at her back as she went to get the standing milker to milk out the marked cows. When she had finished with them, she poured some of the milk into four calf buckets and handed two to Dan. There were eight calves to feed and she laughed at Dan's expression when each one butted the pail and grabbed onto the big nipple. The look of intense concentration of each calf's face made him laugh. When he almost lost his grip on one pail when the calf butted it so hard that the pail swung backward, Dan grinned at her. It took only seconds for each calf to gulp down the milk, and they went back and filled the pails again and repeated the process with the other four calves.

By the time they had washed the pails and nipples, cleaned the calf pens and put down fresh bedding, the main herd had been milked and Pete was flushing the system.

"I thought Erin and Eric had the easy job, feeding calves, but obviously I underestimated what they did,"

Dan commented as they walked toward the big door. Lydia found Pete in the milk room, checking gauges and taking milk samples from the tank. "If you need me, tell Irving to call, Pete. I'm really glad you could come to work for Irv. He needs you, you know."

"Yes, he does," Pete agreed. "And the cows need me too," he added, pausing to label the sample bags. When he looked up at her, his expression was knowing. Lydia nodded. There would be no need to worry about Irv's cows on Pete's watch.

Lydia climbed into the SUV and stretched her arms over head, pressing her hands against the roof. "Okaaaay. Let's go find the twins and go home."

"I'm ready," Dan agreed. He could see Pete backing the manure spreader up to the far end of the barn and heard the rattle of the gutter cleaner. "Pete has everything under control, doesn't he?" He watched as the man hopped off the tractor and walked back into the barn.

"Looks like," Lydia agreed, pulling out onto the road. "He may be the best thing that's happened to this farm in twenty years. If Irv will let him take over enough to make a difference, things should look up. He's a good man, according to my father. Certainly, the cows will be better off," she added.

"I'm going to get cleaned up and change and maybe work some more on the book before dinner, Lydia." Dan looked at Lydia, dressed in grubby jeans and a

T-shirt, her hair tied back in a ponytail, and she looked beautiful to him. She had drive, determination, integrity, and kindness all mixed in the same package. He wanted it all, he admitted to himself.

He looked over at Erin, who was already separating eggs, dropping the yolks into one bowl and the whites into a big mixing bowl. He could tell that Erin had been watching him stare at Lydia. Great, his love life was being scrutinized by a kid!

Lydia walked over and hooked her arm through his and he walked out to the porch with her. She pulled him around the corner, out of sight of the kitchen, and wrapped her arms around his waist. Dan didn't waste a second before he was pulling her tight against him and kissing her long and hard. He was breathing rapidly when he released her and she reached her hands up to his face, rubbing her thumb against his dimple when he smiled at her.

"Go write your book," she said, rising up on her toes to place feathery kisses on the corners of his mouth. "Dinner's at seven. Come back whenever," she said, leaning back against his arms. He slid his hands up to her shoulders and then released her.

"What's your plan for tomorrow, now that you don't have to be up at four in the morning?"

"I intend to sleep late. Mom and Dad should be home by dinnertime, so I guess I'll have to straighten up some of the mess I've made." She could feel his silent laugh as he bent his head to kiss her. When she came up for air, she leaned back against his arms, smiling.

"Okay." Dan nodded. "I've got to spend the day on the book, though. Editors get testy if you don't make a deadline." He rubbed his hands up and down her back, and she sighed. "I've got to go now, Lydia. You're much too tempting."

"Good." She paused for a second before asking, "Like you're not?"

He laughed before he kissed her again and then pulled away, turning to pick up his laptop from the table. Lydia followed him to the steps and watched as he started down the path. Then he turned around and walked backward, smiling at her until she was out of sight.

Lydia stood there for a minute before she went back inside. Erin flashed her a knowing look, which should have been out of place on a fourteen-year-old face, but wasn't. "I hope I find someone like him when it's my turn," she commented as Lydia walked through the kitchen. "Yeah" was all Lydia could think to say. Yeah to an honorable, strong, kind, loving man. She wandered down the hall and climbed the stairs to her room. Ten minutes later, she was still standing in the middle of her room, doing nothing. The sounds from Eric's CD player broke the trance she seemed to be in and she finally gathered clean clothes, kicked off her sneakers, and went into the bathroom to shower.

Chapter Twenty-one

It rained heavily during the night, leaving puddles in the farm lane. The sound of the quad's engine slowly increased until it was close enough for Dan to see the machine coming from the farthest pastures. It wasn't quite seven in the morning and somebody was out checking the animals already. The thunder had been loud and the lightning strikes close during the storm, but now the sky was clear, the air cool and dry.

The quad and its rider swung around the barn and headed up the drive to the cottage. Dan left the porch and walked toward it, hopping on the back when Lydia slowed down. "Good morning to you," he said into her ear as he moved forward on the seat until his thighs cradled her hips. He grabbed for the extra helmet as she revved the engine and took off around the cottage and turned smoothly onto the driveway. He could hear her laughing as she increased speed and he reached around her and gripped his hands together against her stomach. When they reached the incline toward the house, she slowed their speed until they were riding sedately up to the back porch.

He pulled his helmet off and reached for hers as she lifted it off her head, before pulling her back against his chest with his other hand and kissing her neck.

"Good morning to you too," she said, laughing again. "Come on in and I'll fix pancakes for breakfast. Don't worry," she added, "they're out of a box. I can hardly ruin them. And we have real maple syrup to go with them."

"I'm convinced," he said, bringing his leg over the seat and backing away so Lydia could hop off. She grabbed his arm and pulled him toward the porch, just as Flirt came ambling up the hill, tongue lolling, sides heaving. "Did she run all the way out and back with you?"

"You bet. Right, Flirt? She likes to keep her skills current, you know," she said, looking at Dan out of the corner of her eye. "Border collies never really quit working. Even when they're old and arthritic, they want to work." She held the door open for the dog and invited her in to get a drink of water.

"Truthfully, I don't know how I can think about food after dinner last night. Erin outdid herself, and," she added, "having Sophie and Kevin was fun."

"It was, and the lemon meringue pie was spectacular," he said, grinning at her as he reached for the glasses.

"You would know. You ate enough of it," she said, smiling as she poured pancake mix into a bowl.

Dan thought that a plateful of pancakes smothered in butter and maple syrup, washed down with a big glass of milk and shared with Lydia made this morning the best of the last couple of thousands. Probably more. Lydia had found that the cows and sheep and their fences had all survived the storm unscathed. She was sitting there, one hand rubbing the dog's head, and he thought about the possibility of starting every day this way. With Lydia.

He carried their plates into the kitchen and had them washed before Lydia even had their glasses to the sink. "I'm going to work on the book all day if I can, Lydia. Anything I can do for you?"

"Well, let's see. You're very good at washing dishes," she teased, "so how about doing the lunch dishes? After you eat lunch," she added.

"Got it. I'll be back," he promised, kissing her lips and tasting the maple syrup. She tasted so good he leaned in for a longer taste, feeling her smile against his lips.

"Mmm. Come back soon," she whispered as she pulled away.

She watched him walk down the lane and stood there for a few minutes, until she heard Eric's footsteps on the stairs. He didn't walk down them, he clattered, Lydia thought, smiling. He'd always been easy to keep track of, even as a little kid, by the amount of noise he made moving from one place to another.

"Pancakes?" she asked as he shuffled into the kitchen. She took the grunting sound to mean yes and poured batter into the pan. He was taller than she was now and he ducked away when she tried to smooth his hair down. She had turned the pancakes and lifted them onto a plate when Erin came in the kitchen. Erin came to stand beside her at the stove as she cooked another batch, holding a plate to receive the nicely browned circles.

"Dan was here already, huh? I saw him walking down the hill when I got up." She lightly pinched Lydia's arm and added, "Can't stay away, huh?"

Lydia ignored her, filling her plate and waving the spatula at her. Erin grinned and went out to the porch where she proceeded to pour enough syrup over her pancakes to saturate them. Eric looked at her plate and uttered a sound of disgust that Lydia could hear from the kitchen.

Lydia was standing in front of the open refrigerator door, thinking about what they could fix for lunch when Erin reached around her. "I took some beef out of the freezer to defrost last night. Grandpa loves pot roast so I'm going to do one in the crock pot. There's a roaster chicken I thought I could cook for lunch, so we could have sandwiches. Okay with you?"

Lydia turned around and hugged her. "You are the best, Erin. Do you need me to do anything before I go clean garlic?"

"Nope. I've got it," she said, lifting the chicken onto the counter. "I'll come down and help you as soon as I get this stuff started. Take Eric with you," she added. "He needs something to do."

Lydia grinned at her and went out to collar Eric. She called Flirt and the three of them walked slowly down the lane to the drying shed. Lydia could see Dan doing push-ups on his porch and remarked that he really worked at keeping in shape. Eric looked at Dan and then at her. "Okay if I go work out with him, Lydia? I'll come back and help, I promise."

He looked like a little kid asking for a treat and Lydia laughed, waving him away, before stepping into the dimness of the shed. By the time Erin joined her, she had a huge pile of bulbs ready to clean. It looked like three hours of work, maybe only two, if Eric pitched in. Erin loaded the CD player with a disc she had brought with her and her favorite Shania Twain songs kept them company while they worked their way through the pile.

Eric's T-shirt was soaked with sweat when he sat down at the table and picked up a toothbrush. "Dan really pushes, you know?" he told Lydia as he lifted a bulb from the pile and started brushing dirt out of the root mass. "He did a hundred push-ups and a hundred sit-ups without breaking a sweat. Then he did 'em again," he added. "That was before we started doing free weights."

Lydia looked at him, smiling. "Were you able to keep up?"

"Not likely," he admitted. "We're going for a run this afternoon before dinner," he continued. "That's okay, isn't it?"

"Absolutely." She glanced at Erin and winked. "You said he needed something to do."

Within two hours, they had cleaned every bulb on the table. Lydia pulled some flattened vegetable boxes out and assembled them, intending to fill them. The music was still loud and the fans still hummed in the background as they carefully filled the first box. None of them heard the screen door bang shut.

The voice that shouted "Hello" above the noise made all three look up. "Dad! Hey!" Lydia called out. His hug could have broken ribs, he squeezed her so hard, and Lydia laughed. "Where's Mom?"

"Unpacking some stuff we brought back for you guys," he said, transferring his grip to the twins. "You guys look great"—his eyes slid to the garlic—"and so does this," he announced, letting go of the twins to examine the bulbs on the table.

"I knew the garlic would bring you home no matter how much Mom dragged her feet."

His tanned face crinkled into a grin as he hugged her again. "She was ready to come home too." He looked around when Eric shut the CD player off. "You ready to quit here?"

"Sheep and cows are fine, and so is Flirt," Lydia said as she watched her father squat in front of the dog and greet her. "How come you're here so early? Mom said dinnertime when she left the message."

"We left at oh-dark-thirty this morning. Mark and Susan send their love, by the way," he said, straightening up.

"Aha. That's where you were." Lydia raised her eyebrows at him and he shrugged.

"I haven't seen Mark in a while. It was time," he defended himself. "And your mother agreed," he added as if that clinched his position.

Lydia rolled her eyes at him as they walked toward the house. Her mother came running out the back door and hugged all of them. Her hair was still the same light brown as Lydia's, pulled back from her face and secured with a clip at her neck. Her laugh lines were visible as she hugged Lydia again and turned to Erin and Eric. "I'm so glad to be back!" she exclaimed. "Let's get some tea and you three can tell me everything that's happened since we left."

"Okay, Mom. I have to deliver some garlic to the farmers market before lunch. You want to come with me?" Lydia was sure her mother had a dozen questions about their tenant and now that she knew they had been visiting Uncle Mark, she knew she wasn't going to escape an interrogation. Better to get it over with, she thought.

They filled her parents in on the happenings at Irv's, and Lydia was vague about what had happened to Billy and Robert. Her father nodded in satisfaction when she told him that Pete Hudson had taken over the dairy.

Her mother slowly sipped her tea and finally put the glass down. "Come on, Lydia. Let's go deliver the garlic."

The box of garlic rested on her mother's knees as Lydia maneuvered the SUV through the village. "Mark said the young man renting the cottage works for DEA. Am I going to like him?"

Ah, the "careful, don't let my twenty-eight-year-old daughter think I'm interfering" method of interrogation. Her mother was not subtle when she wanted information, Lydia thought. Uncle Mark had probably told them everything known to the Western world about Dan and his family, so she had cut to the chase and just asked, "Am I going to like him?"

"Yes." Lydia laughed.

"That's it? No explanation?"

"None," Lydia said. "You'll decide for yourself. You know, Mom, that you've never let anyone else's likes or dislikes influence you.

"Hmm. I take it that means you like him."

Lydia didn't answer, concentrating on pulling across the traffic into the farmers market entrance.

"Never mind. I'll find out," her mother said.

Lydia lifted the box from her mother's lap, leaned farther over and kissed her cheek and admitted, "You've never failed yet."

Matthew glanced up from the pile of mail on the table as he heard the porch door open. His brother had given him a very accurate description of Dan Madison: calm, confident attitude, steady brown eyes, athlete's movements.

Dan hesitated in the opening, scrutinizing the man seated at the table. This was obviously Lydia's father, home early. He had the same eyes, a cool blue-gray, looking at him now with friendly interest.

"Come on in," he said, standing and extending his hand. "Lydia and her mother will be back in a few minutes. Have a seat."

"I'm Dan Madison," he introduced himself. "I'm renting your cottage."

"I know. Mark's description was very accurate. I'm sure I know too much about you and your business, but you can relax. You're very welcome here."

Dan grinned at him, sinking back into his chair. "Thank you, sir. I've enjoyed my stay and the opportunity to get to know some of your family."

"From what Mark said and what Lydia didn't say, I gather your interest is mainly in one member of my family," he said, raising one eyebrow. "I really don't want to know anything more," he said, smiling slightly, "but beware of my wife. She's better than a CIA operative when it comes to gathering intelligence." Dan laughed when he added, "She taught high school for thirty-five years."

Dan studied the calm face turned toward him. "I expect you know something of what's going down here." At Matthew's nod, he went on. "Lydia figured it out pretty quickly and has been involved more than she should be. I don't think she's in any danger," he reassured her father, "but I can't be absolutely certain that no one has made her connection to me a cause for concern," he said carefully.

"Sometimes too much education can get in the way of common sense, but I doubt that's the case with Lydia. She won't do anything to put you or herself at risk." He turned his head at the sound of a car in the driveway and stood up. "Come meet my wife. I'm sure she's already grilled Lydia." He laughed.

After a lunch of chicken sandwiches on fresh bread, Dan stood up to leave. Lydia's mother had been very discreet and very thorough in her questioning. Matthew just grinned at him in commiseration and Lydia had laid her hand on his thigh under cover of the table. Anne Glenn's resemblance to his division chief ended when she hugged him before he left. Lydia walked out on to the porch with him, and he pulled her around the corner of the house, kissing her as soon as he was sure they were out of sight.

Lydia was laughing when she stepped back. "See you later, Dan? Mom's finished with you. You'll be safe," she teased.

He pulled her back into his arms, kissing her lightly. "Yeah. I found a problem in the plot and I've got to finish fixing it this afternoon. We could go to town later, if you want," he said hopefully. "I'm going to need a big break by four o'clock."

"You're on. I know where we can get the best Coke float in the entire state," she grinned.

With a quick kiss, she turned to go back in the house and he walked down the lane, forcing his thoughts to the plot that wasn't quite right and how to fix it without having to rewrite the entire second half of the book. It would be good to get this out of the way now so he could concentrate on what he was pretty certain would be tomorrow's scenario, the final phase of this operation.

Kissing Lydia when she tasted of chocolate ice cream was as delicious as kissing her tasting of maple syrup. In fact, he mused as he changed into running shorts and a ratty T-shirt, kissing her was addictive and requiring a bigger dose every time. He shook his head. He'd been chasing druggies too long if he was describing the experience of kissing Lydia in drug terms. He heard Eric come up the steps and knock on the door, and Dan walked out of the bedroom with his running shoes in his hand.

An hour later, Dan walked back toward the cottage, his breathing returning to normal, and the sweat drying on his skin. His cell phone vibrated against his hip and when he pulled it free, saw Kevin's number on the readout.

The takedown was set for tomorrow. Kevin would be there at ten in the morning and they would coordinate the plan with the operation's boss by phone.

Good, he thought, disconnecting. It was almost over. The waiting was always the hard part, and now that was over.

Chapter Twenty-two

The remainder of the Mobile Enforcement Team was there, ready and waiting. The distinct sound of a seaplane approaching captured everyone's attention and Dan and Kevin, both dressed in black with Kevlar vests under their DEA jackets, squatted low under the edge of the embankment next to the runway.

A hundred feet away, two more agents made themselves invisible as the plane taxied to a halt next to the fuel pump. The pilot was alone in the cockpit and climbed out the far side and straight into the arms of a DEA agent, who seemed to pop up from nowhere. Dan had seen him move out of hiding as soon as the engine's whine wound down and the pilot was distracted by the routine of shutting down.

Dan and Kevin moved into place, weapons drawn,

before the pilot really registered what was happening. Two sheriff's patrol cars cruised up, disgorging four uniformed officers, all looking like they had itchy trigger fingers. Dan spotted Butch Fraleigh among them and moved to stop him from climbing into the plane. "Agent Farella is here to do the search, Butch. He's a specialist in this kind of thing," he explained, a hand on Butch's arm. Butch looked at his hand resentfully and pulled his arm away, but allowed the DEA agent to climb into the plane.

The pilot had been searched, handcuffed, and read his rights. The familiar-shaped package had been found in his jacket pocket and secured before Kevin stopped next to Dan, putting his gun back into his shoulder holster. "Nice. Not a shot fired. I like that," he confided. "Your friend Butch wanted to be the one searching the plane, didn't he? Glory seeker, you think?"

"Yeah. He'll be running for sheriff in a few years. It would look good on his record, I guess." Dan grinned. "Too bad."

There wasn't anything else for them to do until later, so Dan and Kevin both left the scene after the pilot had been loaded in a patrol car and driven away. The agent in charge made arrangements to have the plane towed into a hangar and secured there, hidden from view, until they could go over it more thoroughly.

The airport was quiet again. The package was in the hands of the DEA and Dan knew they intended to plant it in the hunting shack, leaving it in the same place as the previous pickups. It was important to make sure that the package was picked up before they moved in to make an arrest. It was too easy to claim an innocent reason for being in the woods in the early morning, and too hard to prove otherwise unless they caught the targets with the goods in their hands.

It was almost dark when Dan walked up the steps to the cottage. He had seen the swing moving slowly and had heard the creak of the chains supporting it and knew Lydia was waiting. He felt a rush of heat in his chest as he climbed the steps and reached for her as she stood up. She was kissing him, little feathery kisses all over his face, and her arms were pulling him tighter, even as he moved closer, until they were touching knees to chest. He stood there, absorbing her, relaxing in her hold. There was no thought in his head of bad guys, guns, or danger. Just Lydia.

When he finally managed to make himself pull away, Lydia sagged against him, her arms still wrapped around his waist. "My, oh my," she whispered.

His thought exactly. He looked down at her, smiling. "Go home now, Lydia. I'll come by the house in the morning when we're done with the next phase." She released her hold as he turned her gently and pointed her towards the steps.

"Okay. See you in the morning." As she went down the steps, she looked over her shoulder. "Keep safe, Dan." As she started down the driveway, Flirt appeared at her side and Dan smiled. Her personal escort was on duty. She turned around to face him. "I love you," she said and turned around again and kept walking.

Kevin was grumbling. It was almost daylight, and they had been in position for two hours already. "Where the hell are these dirtbags?" he muttered under his breath, shifting slightly to ease his leg. The early-morning sounds continued, with the birds making their usual racket.

A voice murmured in his ear at the same instant that the woods became quiet and he reached to adjust the head set. The voice giving them the heads-up cut in again. The target was a thousand yards from their position and closing slowly. Dan heard the sound of the engine then, coming closer by the second. He and Kevin were paired, ready to move in on the vehicle as soon as the passenger had entered the shack. Two other agents were inside the shack, ready to make a move as soon as the pickup man had the package in his possession. Sheriff's deputies were outside the shack, hidden in the brush. A pair of agents was following the vehicle in, moving through the woods parallel to the dirt track, to prevent the driver from trying to flee.

The black SUV halted in its usual place and the passenger exited, leaving the door open. The same man, wearing the same sports jacket, walked toward the shack, his weapon drawn. Dan and Kevin moved up on the vehicle from the rear. Dan held his Glock ready as

Kevin entered the passenger's side, pointing his weapon at the driver. The driver's door was whipped open and Dan had his gun pressed up against the driver's neck before he could roll out of the seat. Kevin secured the weapon from the guy's hand and had him cuffed and shoved out on the ground before he could make a sound.

There was the sound of a gunshot from the shack and they both dove behind the SUV, dragging the prisoner with them. "Man, I hate it when they start shooting." Kevin's comment sounded loud in the silence. The two agents, the DEA lettering standing out against their dark jackets, emerged from the shack and bent over the man writhing on the ground. When the sheriff's deputies and two other agents converged on the downed man, Kevin stood up and looked down at their prisoner. "Gotta get shot to get any attention around here." He reached down and slapped a cuff around one ankle and then reached underneath the SUV to lock the other around the rear axel. "You'll keep for a while," he said, looking down at the prone figure. He looked at Dan and then slapped him on the shoulder. "Nice job. Too bad you're retiring."

Fifteen minutes later, an ambulance came up behind them and then edged around the SUV. Dan followed it while Kevin babysat their man. The agents and sheriff's deputies backed away while the paramedics examined the man on the ground. He spotted Butch Fraleigh and walked over to stand next to him. Butch glanced at him and nodded toward the downed man. "A leg wound. Looks like it hit the femur. He won't be walking for a while but he's already talking."

The paramedics dressed the wound, splinted the leg, and loaded him into the back of the ambulance. Two sheriff's deputies, including Butch, got in the back with him and the doors were closed. The agent in charge walked back to the SUV with Dan. "You got the guy secured?"

"No problem, sir," Dan assured him. "He hasn't said a word yet," he added.

"Let's get this one out of here," he said, signaling a deputy to bring in a car. "You two get your reports ready and bring them with you for the debriefing this afternoon. Three o'clock," he added. "One of you stay until the tow truck gets here to pick up this SUV," he said, looking at Dan.

Kevin was on his cell phone before the car was out of sight. When he closed it, Dan looked at him curiously. "Just calling for a ride," he said, winking. "You sure you want to give up this exciting life, Dan? It's not every job that let's you take down the bad guy before dawn and then go meet a beautiful woman for breakfast."

"I think I'll stick with the part about breakfast with a beautiful woman and leave the rest to you, Kev." Dan grinned at his friend. "I think I can manage to live without the adrenaline rushes."

"Whatever. You wanna pick me up for the debriefing?" Kevin flashed a look at his watch and said, "Oops, gotta go. She's picking me up out on the highway in ten minutes."

"Yeah. Give Sophie my regards. Don't forget to take the rest of your gear," he added as Kevin started to walk away.

"Oh, yeah. Right," he said veering off to grab his pack from behind the tree where he had stashed it.

Dan laughed. He couldn't help it. This was the first time he had ever seen Kevin in a state over a woman. Now, if only the tow truck would get here and take this SUV to impound, he could get out of here. He had business to finish and a woman to kiss.

Lydia had been reading since five A.M., a standing lamp providing the light shining on the pages of her book. She had chosen a cozy mystery, knowing that she wouldn't be able to concentrate on anything much heavier while she waited. The wicker settee on the porch was comfortable and she had taken some of the pillows off the other chairs and was propped against them in the corner, her legs stretched out.

It wasn't quite dawn, the sky just barely brightening, when she heard leather slippers scuffing the tile floor in the kitchen. She hadn't left a light on in there but didn't need to see to know it was her father. He came out onto the porch and sat down next to her when she pulled her knees up to make room. He didn't say anything, just patted her foot. She could hear the sounds of the coffeemaker in the kitchen and, when it stopped, he got up and went inside. He came back a minute later with two steaming mugs and handed one to her before sitting in one of the wicker chairs.

It was just dawn when they heard the crack of gunfire, one shot, then silence again. Her father leaned toward her and squeezed her arm and then sat back. He didn't say anything and neither did she.

There was a sound from the kitchen and Lydia looked up to see her mother stepping out onto the porch. She leaned over and hugged Lydia and then came around and sat next to her. Matthew offered her his coffee mug, but she shook her head.

The sun was rising when her mother looked over at her. Her book was forgotten in her lap and she couldn't remember anything she had read. "He's here," her mother said, reaching over and pressing her hand against Lydia's arm.

Her mother got up and pulled Matthew to his feet. "Your hearing is better than anyone I know," he said, glancing out the screens and seeing a figure walking toward them.

Her parents disappeared into the house as Lydia jumped up and walked out the door. Dan got to the steps just as Lydia hit the bottom one and she had her arms around his neck and was kissing him all over his face before he could drop his pack. He staggered back slightly, wrapping both arms around her and lifting her off the step and against his chest. "A fine welcome home for the warrior," he teased just before he brought his lips to hers. He continued to kiss her as he let her slide down his body until her feet touched the ground.

He moved his mouth to her ear and whispered, "I heard what you said when you left last night, Lydia. I love you, Lydia, forever and for always."

Lydia stood there, wrapped in his arms, her face nestled against his neck, loving him.

mL

$\dfrac{5}{10}$